The Swan
and
Arrow

At The
Sign of the Swan
and
Arrow

J. Carter Merwin

Other books by J. Carter Merwin

The Tales of Earden Series:
The Swan and Arrow
The Fledgling
The Guardian and the King
The Seer
The Key and the Bee Hive
Hobb's Lake Secret
Lazarus

Acknowledgements

First and foremost I would like to thank my sister-in-law Eileen for her boundless creativity and encouragement over the years (bookbogglers.com) and to Trevor Lockwood of Braiswick Publishing for his patience and efforts on my behalf.

Thank you to my enthusiastic co-workers at the Rutland County Humane Society of Vermont for their good-humored support of my scribbling. Thank you to Judy Sutherland for being my first 'reader and advisor' and to "Momma Sue" Smith, my cheerleader.

Thank you to the Tom Smith Writer's Group, we will miss his guidance and his humor, to Joyce Thomas, Megara Fitch and Martha Molnar for their help and encouragement, especially on the third book, "The Guardian and the King".

Here are two websites I would like to acknowledge that were helpful in my research:
www.sammyfranco.com and www.thestir.cafemom.com

Finally, all my love and thanks to my family, and especially to my dear husband Tom without his love, support and patience my adventures would never have been begun.

Dedicated to "The Professor"

A List of Characters

Aolwynd – A girl who lives on the western coast of the land of Earden, near the great seaport of Saels.

Gerda – Aolwynd's over-protective nurse/housekeeper

Folpas Melior – spice and precious goods merchant and sometime scholar, widowed father of Aolwynd

Lord Boru – Young captain of a troop of Guardians, (the soldiers of Earden), son of the Supreme Guardian, ruler of Earden

Jorus – Folpas' gardener

The Banker – a pirate

Lord Faolan – Lord Boru's younger brother

Halduro – Councilor General in the army of Earden

Lord Borchard – The Supreme Guardian, ruler of Earden, seated in the capitol city of Guardia, Boru and Faolan's father

Fila – a tavern maid

Jem – a fisherman of Saels

Mam – his old mother

Brilla – a young woman training to be a healer in The House of Good Women

Lauro – The Matron of The House of Good Women of Saels

Table of Contents

Prologue - Always Disobeying pg. 11

Chapter One - The Promise pg. 15

Chapter Two - Kissing a Shadow pg. 27

Chapter Three - The Strong Box pg. 39

Chapter Four - The East Gate pg. 53

Chapter Five - Not a Priest Nor a Jailor pg. 75

Chapter Six - Clumsy Poetry pg. 85

Chapter Seven - The Twin Gods of War pg. 97

Chapter Eight - A Morsel of Poison pg. 117

Chapter Nine - Faolan's Glove pg. 127

Chapter Ten - Hearts are Fools pg. 137

Chapter Eleven - Sage and Mistletoe pg. 147

Chapter Twelve - A Loop of the Rope pg. 155

Chapter Thirteen - A Note Sealed With Wax pg. 165

Chapter Fourteen - Olive, Almond and Sesame pg. 175

Chapter Fifteen - Rose Petals,
                    Sandalwood and Flames pg. 183

Chapter Sixteen - The Underworld pg. 197

Chapter Seventeen - "...All in the Head." pg. 203

Chapter Eighteen - Warriors and Givers of Life pg. 215

Chapter Nineteen - Dark Arts pg. 223

Chapter Twenty - Three Little Graves pg. 231

Chapter Twenty one - Fashioning a Noose pg. 241

Chapter Twenty two - With the Blade Uppermost pg. 251

Chapter Twenty three - By A Loop of Ribbon Bound
                    pg. 261

Chapter Twenty four - "Would You Follow Me...?" pg. 269

Fear walks with Courage
For they are brothers
And both are blind.
If Fear goes first
And Courage follows after
All will be well,

But if Courage goes first
And Fear
Comes up behind
Both will be lost.

From
The Battle Scroll of Earden

Prologue

"From a casement window, that is how I first caught the gleam of his armor and shield in the morning sun. I was only young, just dressing for the day when a cool breeze came in through my bed chamber window making me shiver, bringing the taste of salt from the sea and the scent of flowers with it. My hair blew across my face of a sudden and I struggled to see clearly, dragging it away from my eyes. My nurse Gerda clucked behind me like an angry hen. "Get away lest the whole world see my naughty child in her shift and rat's nest of hair!" I can hear her dear voice shouting at me. How I miss her now. As a wild young girl however, my greatest pleasure was to stoke her anger. Disobeying, I leaned further across the deep stone sill. Was I always disobeying? It seems so now.

Then I saw my captain for the first time riding beside his troop of men. Hearing his voice upon the wind, struck from that instant, I was in love. I know it may sound silly...a girl of thirteen, what could I know of love? But there he was and something tugged at my heart like a cord. He was also young, greener than the men he lead, yet his confident laughter carried strong across the hills and into the valley where my father's villa stood. The rattle of their shields and the sounds of horse's hooves grew loud and blended with the whipping of their many banners. As they rode past our gate the standard bearer was at his side. He wore the surcoat of the Guardians of Earden with its spiral emblem picked out in silver studs upon a field of dark green. His breast plate glinted blue in the sunlight. It hurt my eyes to gaze upon it but I could not look away. Smitten, I tried to memorize the crest tracing it with my finger upon the stone of the sill. His face was merry and yet fierce and his hair blew in the wind about his shoulders. I trembled as I watched him and thought him the handsomest of men. It was clear that this was what he loved best to do in all the world: sword and shield in the service of his country, on some errand of state or battle. So far apart he was from my little world of dogs and cats, gardens and kitchen chores that after Gerda told me his name I dissolved into tears.

I remember then he moved his shield as if it chafed him. Then putting his hand above his eyes he looked about grinning, pointing forward toward the coast at a spot I knew was the first glimpse of the sea.

'Tha's Lord Boru that is...' I remember Gerda saying with a snort as she looked at my cow eyes, 'Tha's the Supreme Guardian's son, and the next ruler of Earden, doon't you bother yerself about him, my girl.'

Thank all the gods he did not see this monkey gawping at him from the window. And thank the gods Gerda's strong arm held me back or I might have fallen to my death and then I would not be here today to tell you my tale...and there is so much more I have to tell!"

1

The Promise

Aolwynd called out to the soldiers from her window, waving madly as only a very young maiden would have dared. Besotted by so much splendor, she grew giddy, her ribs aching from the stone of the sill but she did not care. She pulled a handful of red geranium petals from a pot and meaning to throw them into the air as she had seen fair ladies do, she tossed them out as far as she could. Alas, her arm hit the pot as she reached into the wind and it went tumbling, breaking with a crash upon the steps below. The noise made the horses nearest the gate dance and spin. The soldiers laughed and pointed but the young captain only looked up at the girl and smiled, never stopping the column in their march.

Aolwynd might have willingly followed her heart then as it flew to his, but punishment was swift. Gerda pulled her away with a sinewy hand. Bundling her into a gown and apron, the old woman attacked the girl's hair with a brush, cursing under her breath all the while.

As Gerda brushed, the girl's mind chased far away. Finally, heart pounding, Aolwynd could stand it no longer. Stamping her feet up and down in readiness, she broke free of her nurse's grasp. With the hairbrush flying across the room she ran past the old woman, down the wide marble stairs and out the front door into the morning sun.

"Come back you hellion! Oh! If your mother could see you now! What would she think of me!" Gerda shouted after her.

Aolwynd watched the company ride off until at last, they disappeared behind the crest of a hill. Beyond that hill and the vast green plain that led to it was the port city of Saels, 'The City of the Sailing Ships' at the very end of the world. It was her father's world: a grown-up place she had been to only on sacred holidays, full of strangers and adventure. For long she stood, sighing, thirsting for another glint of armor. But they were gone. Clinging to the branches of the pear, the wind from the sea in her face, her dark eyes tearing up and her black hair all undressed and wild: she remained in a kind of dream. Deaf to Gerda's curses and the laughter of the serving maids who had spilled out into the courtyard, she stood on tip toe until she was lifted down from her perch by the gardener's boy.

From that day onward and from that very hour, as the swans flew north over her city of Saels she made a child's oath, so easy to make, yet so difficult to keep. Aolwynd promised never to love another and to follow Boru, Captain of the Western Guardians and Lord of Earden to the end of her days.

This same road to and from the sea port carried many travelers on the first leg of their journey anywhere, whether they went north, to the wilds, of the Black Mountains, south to the desert lands or to the capital of the realm, Guardia, with its green roof tiles decorated with dragons far beyond the Middle Mountains. Season after season, aching with boredom, Aolwynd stood high in her 'watch tower', the pear tree, waiting for news, stories, wayfarers and soldiers. It was her favorite pastime and her only escape from chores, duties and Gerda's constant instruction in the 'womanly arts'.

Pilgrims leaving the Mother Temple, their cloaks and leather garments stained with salt from sea water offerings and peddlers with their packs waved as they trudged along but they would not stop to answer her questions. Merchants, headed for the city, their wagons heavy, called out greetings to their friend and fellow, the worthy Folpas, Aolwynd's father. Folpas made frequent trips to the harbor to oversee his ships and to oversee   his warehouse on the harbor's edge but he never took her with him. 'Too dangerous', he said. Sitting beside the driver, arriving home, he would cast his glance backwards, across the laden wagon then smile up at his only child, perched on the wall, a promise of foreign and exciting stories to be told her at their fireside. Folpas' trade, and it was a wealthy one, was in rare fabrics, pepper, cinnamon and other spices and exotic stuffs brought from far off lands.

Travelers of the Eastern Road daily kept her spirits alive during the warm months, away from the boredom of everyday and the weight of female drudgery. But the winter seas she cursed when they came, for the road was empty, soldiers rarely patrolled, their campaigns over until the thaw and the harbor was empty of   trading ships. Folpas would spend this precious time in his study amongst his collection of scrolls, smoking his pipe and trying to concentrate. Aolwynd would plop down on the hearth beside his fire and play with the ears of their hounds till her loud and annoying sighs became too much for her father to bear. Frozen with cold she would wander outside, till the scolding of her nurse's voice, as sharp as the winter wind drove her back indoors.

With the spring, travelers, trade and horsemen would be on the march again. As she passed her fifteenth year, she abandoned the pear tree and the wall as undignified to a woman of burgeoning beauty. Instead she took to malingering at the gate, then, growing bold, to stand just outside, in the shadows, ever wary of being caught by Gerda. There she waylaid travelers and begged for tales and news, stories of distant places and especially of the capital of Earden, which filled her head with dreams.

After a time, she dragged a garden bench to just within the wall and all of an afternoon and from then on had brief companions, taking their ease, drinking thirstily from the well, repaying her kindness with tales and song. Soon word spread of a friendly house where one might water your horse. Tables and benches were scattered about the courtyard by her order.

At first Folpas took little notice of Gerda's warnings, of these strangers watering their horses or lounging about his yard for he was a busy man and seldom at home. He called laughed at the old housekeeper called them all 'my guests' and Aolwynd's courtyard 'her little pilgrim's garden'. But when he found his daughter sitting with a young man, listening to him   sing a sad song of elves and   moonlight, Folpas suddenly saw her as any other man might do and he began to worry for her safety. After that, the male servants were instructed to watch over his growing girl and the gate was shut before sunset. Folpas warned his daughter that all this must stop but Aolwynd would not listen. The household would often hear Folpas coming home late from his warehouse, cursing as he tripped in the dark over bundles left behind or bumping into benches left askew.

Ah! Folpas the Sweet (for he always smelled of spices), Aolwynd was ever able to bend him round her finger. "The only daughter of a widow must be spoiled, it is written somewhere...one of my scrolls..." he would say indulgently and with resignation. He knew there was little hope of changing her or even curbing her will as her steps quickened toward womanhood. "You've chosen a very stubborn and singular path indeed..." he would complain, kissing her forehead, "just like your mother."

To this she would agree and wheedle, that her visitors "...were only there for my own amusement," and "the servants are with me, you needn't worry, and then there are my hounds to protect me." She would put her finger in the button hole of his jacket and twist it looking up innocently into his eyes. Folpas would jerk his chin toward their lazy, over-friendly hounds comatose in the sun. "Those? They will protect you? Upon the grave of your mother...only water for your guests, my girl, and nothing more...then show them the gate." At this she would kiss his cheek and dance triumphantly away.

If her father was benignly neglectful, Gerda was not. She did not approve of these vagabonds littering up the courtyard. She was the queen of his household to everyone, and always thought of the house and its family as her own: her Aolwynd, her 'Good Master', her kitchen. Hers to rule and hers to protect. When she swept outside, she would curse under her breath amongst the benches and shout, "Get out of my dirt, you loafers! Be on your way!!" Even the dirt belonged to her. Ever she watched from the doorway, arms crossed like a sentry or peered out the kitchen window. She counted the cups at the end of the day, judging everyone as if they were thieves. She came to be known as "The Bitch Who Growls" and "The Watchdog". Guests would pat the heads of the hounds beneath their table and throw knowing grins toward Gerda who stood or swept, constantly on the watch.

Berating Aolwynd for being so foolhardy, at Gerda's command, Jorus, the gardener took on yet another duty, that of removing anyone the housekeeper did not think worthy of a sit down and a drink of water. Most guests did not stay long when she was about, begging just a cup to quench their thirst before they moved on.

T he long hours of youth passed happily for Aolwynd, listening to tales of corsairs and pirates out of the south, the wolf men of the north and from the east she had stories of the guardians and their battles with giants.

As she bustled about the tables it gave her a grown-up sense of purpose. The courtyard was her domain and these were her subjects. A picture in her mind began to form of who she was, what she might accomplish in her life, that she owned this place of welcome she had made and it 'owned' her in some way.

Gerda scolded this "puffed up chit of an innkeeper" as she called her and mocked her daily as she passed, shouting "More ale, innkeep!" or calling her "Queen of Dishrags" or "Queen of the Washing Up". To Gerda, Aolwynd was made for more than a serving girl and it grieved her to think of Aolwynd's mother, the elegant woman who had died giving her birth. Gerda had promised then to look after this wayward girl and bring her up a lady...not a tavern maid! "Upon my oath!"

But the years passed and   it happened that soldiers also

frequented this friendly house. This was also part of Aolwynd's purpose in opening the gate, though she would not admit it to herself. Her childhood oath, a little embarrassing and almost forgotten, lay waiting like a small burning coal, beneath the ashes.

Late in the spring, with the trees on the hillside all in bloom, a certain company of soldiers finally came riding. Oh how swiftly this coal burned bright again. She held her breath, watching at her gate for that one flash of metal on the green horizon, the tall standard of Earden flying and Lord Boru riding beside it. What would he look like? Had he changed?

Yes, time changed for everyone and Aolwynd was growing up, or so Gerda reminded her constantly. She sang now a shrill tune day after day of lonely, childless females confined to servitude in other people's houses. The praise of marriage was an ever repeated chorus. Gerda would push her to a pane of glass or a mirror and force Aolwynd to look at herself. Aolwynd followed the nurse's hands with humor as they pinched in her waist and pushed up the front of her bodice to emphasize her budding figure. "Why, I was married two years younger than you are now and already had my first child!"

" Child bride you must have been...did the baby live?" Aolwynd grumbled.

" You're a bitter girl and no mistake to say such a thing! Stubborn! Willful! You're poor mother! She'll see you end up in the gutter and I will have to tell her at the end of my days that I failed you! Time to give over playing queen to this constant stream of filthy beggars and give me back my girls!"

For now the Aolwynd's courtyard had become a favored stop on the road and the servants were required by Aolwynd to serve small meals and ale. Her 'special guests' were willing to pay and some offered gold. Gerda railed against their waiting on this 'trash from the highway' instead of cleaning and tending to the house "...as they ought to be doing!" She also resented anyone 'taking' food from her larder, even if they paid for it.

This was getting out of hand but Folpas was busier than ever and when he came home, he looked grey and exhausted, too tired to listen, too tired to do anything but disappear within his library and shut the door.

From Aolwynd's pilgrims came ever more tales of pirates and the brigands who lived in the bare scorched lands of the south. The countryside was growing more dangerous every day with cut throats and other desperate people lurking about. Little time now did any traveler have to while away in her courtyard. All had business elsewhere and to reach the safety of their destination was uppermost in their minds.

Because of these fell times, Lord Boru and his company of horsemen patrolled more frequently about the provinces, especially the sea and mountain villages and finally to Saels which took them past her gate at least twice before winter.

When they arrived Aolwynd would make Jorus bring up water from the well and fill the horse trough while she brought mugs of mead from the cellars. She brought a goblet of wine for the captain herself, while avoiding the evil eye of Gerda. In a panicky excitement, all clumsy arms and legs, she rushed back and forth. She listened, wide-eyed, mouth agape, to the soldier's stories   **of** exaggerated battle prowess and their sarcastic retorts to each other. Drunk with admiration she stood in their midst, tray hanging by one hand at her side. They joked and lied about themselves for her benefit and she loved them for it.

Gerda let out a snort of disgust at this and stomped up

the steps into her kitchen.

With Lord Boru however, Aolwynd's demeanor was grim and brazen. Gripping his goblet with both hands she presented it to him as if it were an offering, arms outstretched like a temple priestess. All would be of a sudden hushed and the men would jab each other in the ribs. Afterward, they quietly teased her and laughed at her angry spluttering. Never did the young captain acknowledge any of the noise around him nor did he even look at her face but holding out his hand, accepted the wine as if he knew it would be there at his fingertips. While he chatted with his men about their journey or their orders he would suddenly grin, reach out and grasp her shoulder near the neck in his strong right hand. Squeezing it tight until she flinched with pleasure and gasped or giggled he would turn her about like a top and shove her away.

The blood pounded in her temples then and she would creep back, standing goggle-eyed behind him, as close as she dared, hanging upon his every word and praying he would touch her again. Never moving or making a sound lest he send her away, deaf to the pleas of his men for more drink. Signaling behind her to the serving girls, they would smile and take over her duties.

She waited half the year to feel this single touch of his hand, to play their 'game' again and then, when he was gone, wait yet half a year more.

Time passed by and her world changed. Darker and darker the tales grew from out of the south. Wars between tribesmen and their kin disrupted the trade between Saels and its neighbors and spilled over into other lands. Cargos of spices and precious fabrics grew fewer. Her father traveled further, boarding ships whose captains he did not know to find goods he bought from tribes in lands he did not trust and his trade fell by half of what it had been.

Sometimes he would not come home at all but sleep at his warehouse and twice in one year, they had no word of his safety for months. His trade was dying and he spent so much time away that he became a stranger amongst strangers in his own home.

In spite of her worries about her father, w   ithout effort, Aolwynd settled into ownership of her courtyard and she began to offer food and drink daily for a price. Many had tried to pay her in the past so in these hard times she held out her hand and accepted their coin with thanks. She found it was easy to do something she had been playing at for years. Aolwynd turned her father's house into an inn and an empty storage barn that used to hold all his goods was turned into a comfortable sleeping hall that smelled strongly of spices. Jorus and his helper cleaned out a small stable, rolled in barrels and tubs and set to brewing mead and honey beer in larger quantities.

Gerda knew not whether to be glad or angry. She was relieved to have 'courtyard' money coming in, of course, but she sighed with bitterness that her hopes for Aolwynd's marriage into a 'proper ancient house' with lineage and ancestors was at an end. Who would have an 'inn keeper' for their lady? A girl grown to womanhood amongst scoundrels and rough soldiers was nothing and no one a proper house would want. Just when she was beginning to 'fill out and blossom' her little girl's prospects vanished like the translucent blooms of the pear tree.

That however, meant the end of Gerda's badgering, for which Aolwynd was sore glad. Aolwynd had offered sweet cakes once to the goddess at the Mother Temple when her father took her into the city. Most girls of marriageable age offered cakes for a handsome spouse and spun their hands in the smoke of the incense for good luck. Aolwynd had smiled at them and nodded, spinning her hands for quite the opposite reason. Freedom.

She had only one regret, her inn had no name, for she could not convince her father to let her hang a sign from the gate. He was now weary with much travel and when he was home he sat in his chair by the fire clinging to memories of better times.

"What do we need a sign for, my beauty?" he would say. "Every vagabond and soldier-boy from here to the Black Mountains knows the way to our door."

It was true, to all who traveled the East Road past Folpas' house, this was a place of welcome where one could find good ale, plain food, friendly company and a bed for the night without bugs.

Gerda kept watch over Aolwynd as always. Even as the serving girls repelled or accepted the busses and good-natured flirting of their guests, Aolwynd glided amongst the tables without hinderance refilling their cups and gathering the news of the day. Gerda watched in wonder at this bumble-bee of a girl, keeping everyone happy, cleaning tables and ordering the servants about.

Life had settled into a pattern that Aolwynd found good. Keeping the inn in theses difficult times was a worry off her father's shoulders. Moving about from kitchen to garden, from cellar to hall, she had no more time for daydreams. Soldiers retreated from her mind like so many forgotten toys. Even Gerda looked on with pride from her kitchen window.

One night, Aolwynd overheard a traveler talking to the man in the cot next to him as she checked the fire in the sleeping hall. He said that this house was known far and wide along the coast as the "Inn of the Swan" and that she was the swan of that name.

2

Kissing a shadow

When the harvest time was over and all the crops at the farms thereabouts were gathered in, a chill wind began to blow and evil came with it. Even so, Folpas decided he must take one more trip to his dockyard warehouse before winter. Aolwynd waved 'Good Journey' to him as he set out. Strangely, that same day, she saw merchant wagons passing their gate in the other direction, going east.

The next morning, a steady stream of gentlefolk, with all their ornaments and furnishings packed around them followed the merchants out of the city. Their servants walked beside the wheels of their carts flashing wide eyes filled with fear. A trader Aolwynd knew from his dealings with her father called out to her from his wagon loaded with family, "Corsairs! Pirates coming up the coast!"

When Aolwynd and the servants stood mouths agape at the news, another traveler shouted to them,   "Sea dogs! Go see for yourself!"

For full a day and a night the wealthy and privileged of Saels fled into the countryside. There were no guests to attend to in this flood of panic for no one stopped to rest but pushed on quickly. Aolwynd ran back and forth to the cliffs over-looking the sea but could see nothing. The servants huddled by the gate and gathered evil tidings, half-truths and bad advice from every group that passed.

After this clot of fat and wealthy citizens, came all those who had the means to hire a cart, or were able to ride away or...run with their hat in their hand.

After that, fell a silence.

" Perhaps it has all been a mistake...I've seen nothing." Aolwynd told the serving girls shooing them away to the house. Then, having no message from her father, she began to worry and took their place at the gate, waiting for her father's return.

In the night came the distant smell of smoke. Something was burning far away. From the crest of the hill she could see an orange glow beyond the dark outline of the city. The harbor or the ships anchored there were on fire! Folpas' warehouse was in that harbor! Folk now flooded up her road in crowds, wild and incoherent. Bleating and babbling they stopped just long enough to tell of the first sighting of the pirate's ships, of the brutality of the mobs, of flames, confusion and terror. How had they come? 'Waiting far out to sea', was the answer, 'stealthily, recklessly swooping into the harbor under cover of darkness' and burning every ship in front of them.

What was she to do? Two more days went by yet her father was neither among the first nor the last of the refugees. Ever she kept watch for him but now through an iron gate locked with a chain. Gerda insisted that she close the doors to everyone. All that could be done was to offer water through the railings to those in need and beg for news of Folpas.

S he learned that the pirates had landed, the soldiers of

the city garrison had fought them, been surrounded and died in their keep, killed by the brigands, ship load after ship load of them. Then the business of hostages began, those unlucky enough to be thought wealthy were gathered up for ransom including several important citizens who had not heeded the warnings. All were being held for gold from those who might pay. But if you thought the city was empty, she was told, you would be wrong. There were those without scruples who holed up in their inns and shops, paying to stay and openly dealing with the pirates. For pirates must drink!

Peeling parsnips with her sleeves rolled up and the shavings dropping into her apron, Aolwynd sat in her courtyard transfixed by the dull orange glow of sunset. Though she knew the fires were no longer burning in the city her fears told her stone walls would not keep them safe for long if the corsairs began to roam.

Rhythmic and steady came the sound of hoof-beats. At first her heart jumped and she thought it might be her father but it echoed along the east road, not from the direction of the city. The road was so dark that she did not see the small company of soldiers until they were already rattling her gate.

A martial voice ordered her to "Open up in the name of Earden!" She unlocked the padlock in a hurry and they threw wide the heavy gates making her jump back out of the way. Dark cloaks covered the riders as they galloped into the courtyard. Their leader jumped from his horse and closed the gates quickly. Grabbing her roughly by the arm he bustled her into the shadows, scattering parsnip peelings and basket across the flagstones. He pounded her wrist against the stone of the wall till she cried out and her little knife fell with a clatter to the ground.

"Is this the inn? We need to commandeer this house!

Who is master here? We mean to take back your city. Can you hide us until the rest of the army arrives? Who is in charge? I must speak to him. Can you keep us secret? Are there any guests here? Is there anyone here who might betray us?"

" Yes...no...I..." She was peppered with questions as his forearm quickly leant across her breastbone forcing her against the wall. Aolwynd began to speak but his gloved hand suddenly covered her mouth. He looked about and pointed to the road. A soldier checked to make sure no one followed them. The leader sighed and relaxed his grip. As he did so, Aolwynd raised her hands in a gesture that meant she could not breath, then palms outward to show she meant no harm. As he took his hand away a stud on his glove grazed her lip. She bit back the pain and wiped the blood with her sore knuckles while trying to regain her composure.

"Speak girl..." he said in a low voice.

" I have no master, my lord. This is my inn and tho' you may not remember it, you have always been welcome here." She spoke softly with just a hint of bitterness in her voice.

He looked at her then, squinting in the darkness and pulled her by the shoulders into the light of the moon now unveiled by cloud. The cool ivy leaves framed her face. Wonder and confusion were in his eyes then recognition sparkled in them. His lips raised slowly in an incredulous smile as he shook his head, confounded. "I cannot believe it. Who is this woman who stands before me? Where is my little shadow who used to follow me about, all eyes and elbows, spilling my ale?"

"Wine."

" Wine, yes. I remember now. You served me wine...and chased after my every want...?"

"I am here, my lord."

"No." he whispered.

"Aye, my lord!" called a soldier, who was listening as he watered his horse at the trough. "Tha's our lass alright, tho' you've nought been here to see! Tha's our Swan an' we're at the inn o' tha' name."

Boru's eyes glowed, or was it the reflection of the lamp from the house? Aolwynd could not be sure. His hands dropped slowly and tenderly from her shoulders down the full length of her arms, as if in close kinship or brotherly welcome. Her skin tingled at his touch. He grasped and held her hands together in his, bending over them and in a voice barely above a breath he said "A swan indeed. Where was I when all this happened?"

"Chasing Wild Men!" the soldier answered.

Her cheeks grew hot and she backed away after gently removing his hands. Turning, she told them to lock the gates then showed them the way to the sleeping hall and to the stable where they might feed and bed down their horses. She left them to settle in and went to the kitchen.

Gerda was sore put out at this intrusion until Aolwynd was sharp with her. After being told who her 'guests' were, she set the kitchen into an uproar creating a mighty supper, fit for hungry soldiers. She called for a spit, a roast of beef and flour for her sesame cakes. She kicked Bror, the kitchen boy to wake him up and sent him out to pick up the parsnips laying and then get to work peeling onions and carrots.

Jorus removed all the benches and tables putting them out behind the inn in the family's own private garden. There he reckoned the soldiers could rest without being seen from the road.

The maids were told to keep their mouths shut and let no light shine at night from the front of the house.

After ordering everyone about, Aolwynd went back to the kitchen to see how things were getting on.

Much in Gerda's way, the captain and his lieutenants were poring over a map of Saels rolled out across her work table. They were deep in concentration as Aolwynd shooed the cat and sat down in the kitchen boy's little chair by the fire closing her eyes. She had not realized how tired she was.

" Who hit you across the mouth, my poor sweeting?" Gerda said with shock in her voice, touching the swollen lip with her floured finger.

Aolwynd waved her away, tired of her fussing. "It's nothing."

Boru lifted his head from the map and peered at her, creasing his brow, then went back to his business.

Gerda stopped what she was doing and cooked an egg. In this way Gerda made everyone in her kitchen know just who she thought was most important. When the egg was ready she made Aolwynd eat it, then brought her a cup of tea.

Its sweet peppermint flavor reminded Aolwynd of her father and she stared into the flames of the hearth as Gerda went back to her roast basting it until it crackled and spit. Aolwynd closed her eyes and leaned back against the warmth of the kitchen wall. She heard Gerda order the men to clear the table. The old woman served supper apologizing imperiously for any dirt on her famous parsnips. They ate as if they had not eaten in days and began to relax, talk and joke as their stomachs filled. Gerda poured them wine again and again. When they had finished they rolled the map back out and resumed their whispered planning.

Aolwynd could see out of half-closed eyes, Boru's own blue eyes intent upon her from across the room. There was no smile on his face. When she had rested, she rose, kissed Gerda on her wrinkled cheek and thanked her for her efforts. She sent the boy to check the fire in the sleeping hall and to make sure the gate behind the stable was locked. She bade the soldiers goodnight and one of them kissed the hem of her apron as she passed him. He pulled off a small piece of peel that had stuck there and popped it into his mouth with a smile.

Gerda raised an eyebrow watching Aolwynd as she left the room. "What's that man's name?" She asked, pointing with a wooden spoon.

"Tanner, behave yourself." Boru said sleepily.

Aolwynd stood in the hallway at the bottom of the stairs looking up at her bed chamber door but instead, slipped outside for a breath of air. The courtyard looked empty without its benches and tables. Lonely. The flagstones in their alternating dark and light pattern shone in the moonlight. She walked to the gate and sighed. Reaching out for the rungs high above her head she grasped them with both hands and arched her back, stretching the ache out of her muscles. It had been an exciting night but a long one and it was nearly dawn. She could not imagine what would happen if what Boru said were true, an army was coming and then a siege. Some fancy of hers imagined men and horses packed into her courtyard like olives in a jar but she knew they would march on to the city and not stop at her inn. "Silly." she whispered smiling to herself.

Soft footsteps came up behind her. Before she could turn, quick as a cat, Boru's warm body was pressed against hers, his mouth against her neck, his arms reaching upward and his hands holding hers to the gate.

" Are you still my little shadow? Are you still smitten with me as you once were, so grown up now, so beautiful? Or was it just as it always is with girls, drunk on soldiers, just uniforms and soldiers…?"

Her eyes saw only the moon, her senses only his heat and closeness, the pressure of his body, pinning her, his breath on her neck intoxicated her. "Well, partly soldiers..." she gulped and tried to speak. "Soldier, I mean, only you… ever." She blushed, amazed at her own frankness. 'Where did that come from?' she wondered and immediately regretted saying it. Gerda had warned her about being honest with men.

Turning her around he lowered her hands. His smile and his grave eyes reassured her. His voice sank to a whisper. "Forgive me for that..." he said, gently touching her lip with his finger.

"It's nothing."

"If I had known."

"That I wasn't just a serving wench?"

"Perhaps."

" Good thing then I wasn't the gardener, you might have killed me!"

" Holding a knife? Yes, perhaps." Boru laughed, still holding her hand as he walked backward into the shadows. The deep scent of cool earth and ivy leaves surrounded them. "I must not be seen, secrecy is all...forgive me for this also."

They sat down on a bench made from the living branches of an old tree. She sighed and lowered her head.

" You are thinking of your father, aren't you? Gerda told us he is missing."

'How is it that the simple recognition of one's feelings can bring one to tears?' She thought.

"Now! My brave girl...my Shadow...stop that." and under his breath he muttered like an old man, "I can't abide a woman's tears!" He lifted up her chin. "We will see it done, we will see it done...dry your eyes." He looked around smiling. "Tell me how I missed you growing more beautiful with these passing years? How many times have I stopped here? I only remember a lot of elbows and knees wrapped up in a dirty apron and an imp who clung to me like a limpet. Not this creature with almond eyes and skin the color of milk!" He licked his index finger and drew a cool line from the hollow of her throat to the cleavage of her breasts. His glance followed it. The night air quickened her skin and her eyes closed for a moment, her head drifting backward, spellbound. It was his turn to sigh. His fingers played with the lacing on her bodice. Wrapping his arm around her back he pulled her close. Holding his breath he took her chin in his hand and with his thumb explored the circle of her lips. It was a demanding caress. He leaned in to kiss her waiting mouth.

A flash of light streamed from the doorway.

" You are too bold, sirrah!" Gerda's voice rang out across the stones of the yard as she marched out of the house. "Aolwynd! Do you know what time it is? Come inside now! There are things...to attend to!"

Boru let go of Aolwynd slowly and leaned forward tracing a pattern with his finger on the flagstone, being careful not to let the old woman see his smile. Raising his head he made a small pout   with his mouth at her protest and Gerda answered him by sticking out her tongue and waving the wooden spoon. She pulled her mistress up from the bench and pushed her toward the house. Aolwynd's head bobbed as she looked back at Boru who had stretched his long legs out and placed his hands behind his head, yawning luxuriously.

Under her breath, just loud enough for him to hear Gerda commanded in their retreat, "You keep your knees together, my girl!"

Boru's head shot up at this and he fell back with a roar

of laughter, his whole body shaking.

When he was alone, his arms resting on his knees, he sat, hunched over in the darkness, thinking. The clouds parted and the light of the moon washed over the stones of the inn. He looked up at its shuttered windows.

3

The Strong Box

Gerda was already making noise early, ordering the servants about as Aolwynd sauntered into the kitchen, yawning. The smell of baking bread and buns with raisins and saffron wafted throughout the house.

Like a sleepwalker, Aolwynd passed through to the larder, running her hand along the crocks on an upper shelf. It would not do to run out of provisions with ten ravenous men about, yet how to get more flour, oil…? There would be nothing to buy at the city's market if indeed it was open at all. Even if goods could be found and the journey safe, buying there would raise suspicion. Everyone knew her inn was closed, so who could she be feeding in such numbers? It was too great a chance to take.

As always, once she began pushing jars and barrels about, she noticed the dust, mouse droppings and cobwebs that even the cleanest households collect over time. She called for a broom and a bucket of warm soapy water.

"Thank you, Bror." she told the kitchen boy as he stood grumpily rubbing his eyes with one fist and holding the washing cloth slack in his other hand like a dead hare.

Soon she was wide awake, cleaning and re-organizing. She ignored Gerda complaints about the dust wafting through to her kitchen. It felt good to be busy and to forget about her fears. Damp black hair strayed in tendrils onto Aolwynd's forehead. She pushed them away with the back of her hand and looked up to find Boru standing in the archway, obediently holding the bucket for her. Bror was back in his chair snoring with the cat in his lap.

Gerda hovered in the background pretending not to be listening to every word.

"Good moro." Boru said, his blue eyes twinkling.

"And to you."

"I see you have set yourself a mighty task."

"Do you need something?" Aolwynd asked peevishly.

"I must see you for a moment...we must talk," he cast a glance behind him and raised his voice for Gerda's benefit, "about our foray, we go tonight into the city."

Aolwynd looked up with alarm. "Of course, of course, just give me a moment. So it begins then?"

Boru smiled.

She wiped her hands on her apron and juggling two saffron buns hot from the oven she followed him out into the sunshine.

"Let us go into your garden, I have let the men sleep as they will need to be sharp tonight." He stretched out his arm like a courtier letting her go first. They walked along a wall where roses were climbing still, even so late in the year, and passed beneath them through an archway. Beds of lilies and asters were clipped down like an old man's beard, all the geraniums so bright with color during the summer months were absent from their pots, only the herbs, sage and tarragon, rosemary and thyme still showed green life. Jorus stood up from a bed and wheeled his barrow out of their sight.

"This is a fine place for solitude." The captain said, sitting down on a bench and stretching out. Aolwynd admired him while pretending to survey her garden. His legs were well-muscled, clad in the worn green leggings of his uniform. His boots were new however, made of a shiny brown leather and they fitted him well. He gazed at them with a smile.

"The garden is yours for as long as you need it. You must have much on your mind." she said pulling her gaze away, lest he catch her.

"Hmmm. What? Yes, always. I will sit here for a while after I tell you of our plans...rather than help you in the larder."

"Sit here as long as you want and admire your boots." she said handing him a saffron bun.

He grinned, nibbled distractedly at it, holding the bun and pointing with one finger at her. "Do you know the city well?"

"Of course. Yes. All my life."

"Good. It is one thing to read a map, quite another to know the streets as they really are. What I have is quite old...I hate maps, they are always out of date. Too many changes, too may surprises. When I am Supreme...I will see to that. But..." He suddenly seemed embarrassed. "Anyway...we will foray tonight and we must slip into the city without being seen...that's why I need your help, we must get out again."

"Let me set someone else upon my 'mighty task', sweeping mouse dropping and we will go over your map together. I love maps."

"Then I will take some pleasure in the task with you to guide me, my lady." He placed his hand over his heart in tribute and looked up at her sweetly.

"No..." Aolwynd looked at him intently, almost angrily. "those bastards! It is my honor to help you if I can, to help my city, to serve my country...I am the one who is honored."

Taking her hand, he stood up and bade her sit upon the bench. A salt breeze stirred the bare branches of the trees. He looked up at the pale blue of the sky and after a pause, cleared his throat. "Forgive me for last night. I have been chastened for my bad behavior by my own men." He smiled and looked about the garden. "You are dearer to them than I knew. After years of coming to this inn, watching you grow...where was I? It is as if I had insulted one of their own daughters...and Gerda...I would not cross that woman and her wooden spoon for all my life!"

Aolwynd laughed and waved away his apology bidding him sit beside her. Something in his warm smile made her bold. She reached out and taking the thin gold cord that cinched the collar of his linen shirt, slowly she undid the bow exposing his neck. Then she stood up still holding the end of the cord between two fingers. Like a puppy dog, he sat enthralled, smiling, waiting. She sighed, feeling the hold she had over him. Time seemed to stop. His lips were parted in anticipation, almost breathless with pleasure. 'So this is what it is like to be a woman...to feel a woman's power over a man' Aolwynd thought, shocked at her own actions but wanting to go further, to see how far she might go, to see if she might control him...play with him, lead him about the yard like a pet on a leash, pull him into the shade and kiss his face, this warrior.

With a shiver at her thoughts and her own brazen behavior she came back to herself or at least to courtesy and let the cord drop. On impulse, stooping over him she whispered as he leaned forward to catch her words, "I will tell you, my lord, if any step you take is not welcome, and as I have already told you, you are welcome here, and always will be." She left it at that and left him also, sitting in the sun. Though she did not turn back to see, she felt his eyes following her.

"You know my lady mother bore me in your city? Yet I do not know it well. My father was loath to let her leave his side after he conquered here and so she never returned. She died when I was only young."

"The Supreme Guardian's history is well known to us." Aolwynd said walking about her father's study. "It is often said that he might have made this city his capital...instead of Guardia." Taking two candle stands from a shelf she placed them on either end of the big leather-covered work table where Boru had already rolled out his map. Going to a cabinet she poured two goblets of dark wine and handed one to the him. Her hounds padded slowly into the room and plopped themselves down on the warm hearth stone where a fire was blazing. They scratched and licked themselves busily, ignorant of any other activity.

Aolwynd leaned over the map of Saels examining it as if seeing her city through the eyes of a stranger. She loved these minute images of the world for they could take her far away, anywhere, to distant lands, even to the constellations of the sky. There were no limits to where she might go in her mind's eye, no limits to distance except the blank spaces where no man had been. When she looked at Boru's map she found first the wide marble concourse at the city's center with its beautiful temples, and the Council Palace surrounding and behind them, the maze of streets and alleys full of shops. "Oh!" she exclaimed. "This has changed! There was a fire here and these alleys have all been blocked off, they were the lairs of cut purses and the council ordered them closed. There is a new entrance here to the

grand plaza..."

Boru laid a hand softly upon the small of her back. "What we chiefly need is a way to enter the city without notice. Cast your eagle eye upon that..."

With a sniff she settled to the task and leaned further over the map. "Let me see...here...no here!" she pointed to a tiny curve in the drawing of the city's southern wall, near the sea, it was only a mark like a little crescent moon, almost a smudge it seemed and might have been overlooked. Boru leaned over as well, still holding his hand on her back but letting it slip slightly lower. Aolwynd shivered and decided not to notice. "This is where they take out the refuse from the lower market at the end of day, I'm surprised it is even on your map, though it is a gate...it has only recently been used for this purpose but now that the farmers are afraid to come into the city, now that the markets have nothing to sell....it will be closed."

"There was no indication, no title written on my map at all, we would not have known to look for it. We would never have known...I thank you." he stood and let his hand slip away. "This will serve us well. What is the manner of the door and its lock, do you know?"

"It is wooden and quite old. I do not think it has a lock, I believe they lean a rock against the door."

"That would change if I were in charge." he said like the young man he was, so sure of improving the world. Stretching his arms, he took up his goblet and stared into the fire. "We will wait until nightfall, then we will see what we will see."

The servants were noisy in the hall and Gerda's busy footsteps resounded on the tiles. Picking up her goblet Aolwynd closed the study door and joined him as he walked to the fire. "When are your troops coming?"

"They should have been here by now...but I am always

impatient."

"Me too."

"Ah." he said finishing his wine and circling her waist with his hands. "I remember a girl who stood behind me by the hour, still as a stalk, her head lolling with sleep, never moving."

"Not very flattering to be compared to a stalk but ever faithful, yes."

"A quality I much admire, in men and dogs." He touched the butt of one of her hounds with the toe of his boot.

"First you hit me in the mouth for greeting, then scatter our dinner upon the stones, now you kick my dogs...what manner of noble are you?" she whispered.

Boru took her by the hand and looking around pulled her toward a comfortable chair. Sitting himself down he slung one thigh over its arm and admired his boot while swinging her hand absently. Suddenly pulling her down he settled her in the warm circle of his legs wrapping both his arms about her tightly. He snuggled his cheek against her shoulder. She let one arm drop limply toward the floor and let the other boldly rest upon his thigh.

They sat blissfully in silence for some time, listening to the heavy breathing of the dogs, the crackle of the fire and the distant noises of the household.

At first she thought Boru had fallen asleep, so soft was his breath upon her neck. All of an instant he bent her forward and laid her across his lap, her head cradled in the crook of his arm like a child. Then his mouth covered hers. The power of his kiss, the warmth of his body and the strength of him overwhelmed her. Vanquished, she had no breath, was weak, the room was spinning. She felt his heart beating against hers. The long years of waiting, all her girlish longing came sweeping back over her and turned at once into a woman's desire. A vision of his armor shining against the green of the countryside rose and the remembrance of her childish oath came so quickly to her that she felt like crying.

He relaxed then, and having conquered, gave a breath of satisfaction, kissing her again, leisurely, playfully. Though his mouth was on hers, Aolwynd could tell he was smiling.

She stood at the gate that night, worrying not just for her father and his safety but also now for the man she loved. Nervously she stalked about while the soldiers readied themselves and their mounts. With every hoofbeat and every clank of their swords she jumped.

Their dark cloaks stood them in good stead for even as she walked amongst them they blended in well with the shadows. Clouds scudded swiftly across the sky and the stars twinkled in the cold air. There would be a frost tonight. Aolwynd rubbed her arms and puffed her breath.

"Go in, you must be cold." Tanner, Boru's second grumbled, echoed by the others.

"No. I will see you off and then start your supper." Her cheery voice fooled no one.

Boru took heed of his men. "We will be late, perhaps all night. Do not trouble yourself, we are not going for a stroll."

She tried to protest.

"Take your fussing elsewhere." he growled.

Chastened, she left them alone. When she looked out the kitchen window they had gone.

It was dawn when she heard the heavy slam of the stable gate and footsteps coming around the side of the house. She quickly threw a shawl over her nightgown and ran down the cold marble stairs, out into the courtyard and around the house to the stable.

Two men half-carried another, who's arms were draped across their shoulders. She stood gaping, almost in tears, counting heads.

"We're all here." A voice came from behind her.

Boru's young face looked tired, his head was bowed, his hair hanging lank across his cheek. She made to touch him but he pulled away. Recovering himself he said, "You're in your bare feet, go back to bed. I need to think."

Late in the morning she and the kitchen boy delivered breakfast to the sleeping hall. They carried trays heavy laden with fresh bread, slabs of butter, slices of ham, berries and cream, stacks of oat cakes, a half cheese and smoked sausages. Aolwynd followed with pitchers of warm cider and mead. Placing all on a plank table outside the doors where they might help themselves, she knocked timidly. Getting no answer she stood like a guilty child for several minutes, waiting, then went back into the house and sat at the kitchen table in a sulking mood.

Gerda crossed her arms in front of her flat bosom and leaned down into Aolwynd's face. Raising her woolly eyebrows, she gave a fierce, slow nod and tipped her head as if to say 'Now you know how men can be.' Aolwynd glared back at her.

The sound of footsteps interrupted this silent women's argument. Boru entered carrying empty trays and set them on the counter before he sat down next to Aolwynd. His face was washed and his mood bright.

"Good moro, ladies. Aolwynd, your gate was there and the stone that guards it." He chuckled. "All went well."

Aolwynd said nothing.

Gerda turned her back to them while crimping the edges of a great veal pie. 'Tsk-ing' with her tongue, she took their dinner to the oven.

"What is this peevish face? I see my Shadow has had

her feelings pricked. Tell me what has offended thee and I will slay the dragon for you." His smile was wide as he stared into her face taking her chin in his hand. He was dressed in a clean green tunic that turned his eyes the same color. His light brown hair swung across his cheek as he leaned forward, forcing her to look at him. "Kiss me and there's an end to it."

'How can I resist him.' she thought, they had all been right to shoo her away.

Gerda huffed scornfully and pulled her wooden spoon closer to her, tapping it on the counter but they paid no attention.

Aolwynd kissed him lightly.

"That's better." he said taking her hand and bending it downward at the wrist in a little gesture. "Take a deep breath, I have news of your father."

Aolwynd gasped.

"Well, rather I have news of the pirates and their captives, none of your father alone but I believe he is there, and I have a plan."

She entreated him with wide eyes to continue and Gerda pulled up a chair scraping it across the floor in her hurry to sit down.

"Do you have gold?"

"Father has a strong box in his study." Aolwynd jumped up at once to get it.

"Wait, wait. Hear what I have to say first. You will need fifty pieces of gold at the very least. Maybe one hundred. The pirates are ransoming prisoners every day at noon on the docks of the harbor. They bring their victims across, those they think will have relations with gold for their release...then they parade them in front of the crowd. If relatives are able to pay, they get their relative back. If no one speaks up from the crowd the dogs drag them back to their ships. The city folk are already resigned to this, the cowards! They stand there like sheep waiting to be fleeced. People gather daily like some cruel festival. We heard talk in the streets last night, they say my father does nothing...they say we've abandoned them." he cursed softly.

Both women were openly crying now. "Please!" Aolwynd said running out of the room and coming back quickly with a pouch of gold."When can you go?"

"Wait, I have more to tell. If at the end of a week no one has come forward to claim these poor souls, they kill them in front of the crowd and throw their heads and carcasses into the harbor. Let us hope your father is still alive and it is not already too late."

"Please...please!" Aolwynd cried, holding her hand to her throat.

Gerda poured herself a brandy and gave one to each of them.

"Thank you for that...Gerda. Here is my plan. Please do not throw me in your oven when you hear it." Then he turned to Aolwynd. "You were so anxious to stay amongst us last night my Shadow, let us test your metal."

Aolwynd stared at him.

He took a breath and bade Gerda sit back down for she had jumped up at this, slammed her cup down, putting both hands on the table. She stared fiercely at him. Boru laid a hand on Aolwynd's arm. "Now, my strong girl, you must go with me, you must drive the cart into the city and you must deal with the pirates."

Gerda spluttered. "She will not! You cannot make her! My dove! My sweeting! Deal with pirates? Never!"

Boru spoke softly. "She must. Her father and this inn are too well known..." he turned back to Aolwynd, "as is the 'Swan' who runs it." He glanced down at the hand he held. "There is just a chance that they know him for the wealthy merchant he is, or his clothes may have made them suspect as much. Either way it bodes well they may have kept him alive for the gold he can bring. Let us hope so. But you must drive the cart and you must be brave. I will be at your side...in disguise."

"Never!" Gerda said pulling Aolwynd up by the elbow.

"When do we leave?" Aolwynd called over her shoulder, squirming with frustration as she was bustled out the door.

"We must go now!"

"You get to your room! I'll not have you do such a foolish thing! Your father would rather die than see you in such danger!" Gerda forced her out of the kitchen and begged Jorus to help. Aolwynd, now angry struggled all the way up the stairs and into her bed chamber. Jorus did as he was bid looking from one woman to the other in confusion. Gerda locked the chamber door from the outside.

Boru leaned against the archway, his arms crossed upon his chest and his head lowered.

"How dare you! You old bitch! My father! I hate you!"Aolwynd's screams pierced the door. Her voice shrilled throughout the house. The serving maids huddled, giggling nervously beneath the stairs.

"Go right ahead and hate me! Who does he think he is? Riding in here, demanding this of us? He may be a princeling somewhere else but he's nothing to me! He's a spoiled, womanizing soldier's brat who's been given a job too big for his new boots and now he needs my girl to help him!"

"Supreme Guardian's brat, if it please you." Boru corrected her under his breath with a crooked little smile on his face.

"She's safe from your paws now, at any rate!" Gerda marched down the stairs in a fury dropping the key into her wizened bosom in front of Boru. Soon pots and pans clattered angrily from her kitchen.

Jorus stood next to him. "No one will want to dig for it there, I'll warrant." He whispered. Boru grinned at him, then he creased his brow looking up the stairs.

"I'll go with ye, never fear." Jorus continued. "Aolwynd slipped me the pouch as we locked her in. P'raps they'll take the ransom from me, I've a reputation of me own in town."

"I'll warrant you have." Boru slapped him on his shoulder as they went out into the courtyard.

4

The East Gate

Jorus brought the cart around to the side of the villa and went back to the stable returning with an armful of old clothes. Boru grinned as he put them on.

"Psssst!"

Boru looked up at the sound. Before he or Jorus could stop her, Aolwynd's legs hung out of her casement window. Flipping around with skirts and petticoats in a twist, her long legs in their grey woolen stockings flailing, she wiggled her way out until she hung suspended like a spider, from the window frame. Boru stood transfixed, admiring the glimpse of pale skin just above her stockings and the blue silk garters that held them up. He came to his senses just in time to move beneath her window as her fingers let go of the frame. She dropped full onto him crashing to the ground. With his arms tight about her hips and his head buried in her skirts, he lay prone, the wind knocked from him. Groaning loudly he pushed her off.

Jorus laughed out loud but Aolwynd signaled him to be quiet. Boru pulled a rose thorn out of his leg as he stood up and offered Aolwynd his hand.

"I'm going instead of you...don't try to stop me." she said looking at Jorus. "He's my father. Give me back that pouch."

Jorus handed it to her.

"Don't say anything to the old woman. He's my father, it's my inn and I'm a grown woman. She can't boss me around anymore. Don't you say anything." She wagged her finger at Jorus. "Don't tell her till we're well away." She turned to study Boru for the first time. "And what are you meant to be?"

Boru looked much less like the dashing young soldier of her dreams than a hoary old peasant. He stood leaning against the cart dressed in Jorus' old clothes, a shapeless felt hat pulled down over his eyes and dirt on his face for good measure. He wore an extra coat which made him look round and heavy.

Jorus helped Aolwynd into the cart shaking his head as she settled her cape about her. He patted her knee and nodded gravely as Boru hopped up beside her. "P'raps ah shouldn't let 'cha but ah know you'd ony run after us. You be careful, girl, seems foolish ta' say it, but she'll kill me if yah doon't come back an I don't relish the conversation we'll be havin' when I tell 'er you've gone."

"When you tell her who'se gone?" Gerda came around the corner wiping her hands on her apron. "Oh! No! Aolwynd!"

Aolwynd clucked her tongue at the horse and snapped the reins decisively without even a glance in her direction. "I'll be back, stop mitherin' me, go back to your pie!" she said with every ounce of courage she could gather.

Gerda glared as they pulled out of the gate.

"You had almost won her over until this..." Aolwynd whispered.

"Aye, that woman is fierce in battle."

"Did you have words before?"

"She cornered me that first night and made me a promise."

"A promise?"

"Yes. She promised to throttle me like a chicken and break a jug over my head if I did not behave myself. When I apologized for my behavior it was more out of fear of her than anything my men might do to me! But now I see you in action, I think you're a match for what ever villain may come..."

The air was crisp as an apple and as they passed the orchards that lined the East Road, Aolwynd noticed with despair that the fruit was falling unpicked from the trees. Deer wandered un-afraid, harvesting all they could eat. The animals looked up with half-closed eyes as the cart drove by.

"Too full to move it seems..." Boru mused. "What meat that would make! Where is my bow when I need it?"

Down the road they went, its course like a pale scar along the edge of the cliffs. The wind ruffled the salt grasses and Aolwynd's hood fell from her head in the wind.

"Leave it down for me," Boru said, "your hair is almost blue in the sunshine. So beautiful." He brushed a strand away from her face.

"You're a sight, really you are." Aolwynd chuckled looking at his dirty face.

A farmer and his wife drove their wagon around them. They had been to the market with goods to sell, much to Aolwynd's surprise. Two children sat grinning in the back. "Get out of the road!" the man barked.

"Look at that dirty old bastard." his wife whispered loud enough for the world to hear.

"Aye. Old Winter and Early Spring..."

"Poor girl! The world's a garbage tip soomtimes an' tha's a fact if a maid like tha's got ta' marry an ol' wreck like 'im."

Aolwynd and Boru held back their reaction with difficulty until the family was out of sight then they doubled over with laughter.

Passing a hedge of scrub pines clinging to the cliffs, they began their descent inland, onto the plain.

The great merchant city of the west suddenly appeared before them. Saels reached out in welcome, its cream-colored walls still dripping with the flowers and vines that made it famous, as if it were a merry place. Its tall towers with rounded rooftops and many bells were all silent now, proving it was not. Thin rivulets of black smoke rose into the sky, indicating random fires in the streets, another sign of the vengeful and vindictive evil that had come out of the sea.

The wharf and the sea beyond could just be glimpsed as they stopped the cart on a crest. It was teeming with tiny figures. Ships with sails the color of saffron in all shapes and sizes choked the harbor.

"Father's warehouse is just there!" she said standing up.

"We'll take this way into the city. There are too many pirates at the Harbor Gate. They like to stay close to their ships, the cowards. Here they will pay less attention to us." Boru pointed to the carts and wagons moving toward the Eastern Gate.

Aolwynd clucked at the horse and they drove down the last slope toward the entrance.

It was true, the farm folk seemed to have forgotten their fear or hidden it beneath their eagerness to take advantage and raise their prices, for there were many carts waiting in a line. Produce was flowing into the city once more and the market places must have re-opened.

"They forgive everything when their stomachs begin to growl." she spat.

"Do you blame them?"

"Traitors."

"Listen my girl, people get hungry, they have children. Pull in your sting, it won't help you now, we are not announcing ourselves at the gate as anyone's saviors, we are being secret now...do you understand?" Boru smiled at her and spoke as if she were dumb as a post, slowly and with emphasis.

Aolwynd crossed her eyes and lolled her tongue out the side of her mouth.

"There's my bright girl...now listen to me, show no anger to anyone, show no fear at anything you might see, feign a cow-like stupidity if you must show anything, it will get us further. Trust me. But not that face, please."

"My hands are beginning to sweat, my heart is pounding." she said.

Boru pinched her arm and whispered fiercely into her ear. "Bank it down like a fire, use it, relish it, don't let your fear run away with your head. Master it. That is the first lesson a soldier learns."

He seemed to be enjoying the prospect of this adventure! On his face was a look she'd not seen before, a reckless alertness in his eyes as he glanced quickly around, taking in everything, and that grin...one he must surely have served to a foe in battle.

"Be brave now, here's your first test coming. Remember, I'm here but I dare not interfere, you are my mistress, I am a doddering, harmless, old gardener along for the ride." He pulled his hat down further over his face and hunched over.

"Hmmm, harmless..." she said rolling her eyes as they pulled into line behind the others. One by one the carts approached the gate and were stopped, their drivers questioned and their goods prodded and poked. It could have been any other market day except for the sullen faces of the farmers and the pirates standing sentry instead of city guards.

Grubby and tattooed, the corsairs were ugly with greasy black hair hanging down beside their ears in braids. Bits of color that might once have been scarves were wrapped about their necks, and their gold earrings sparkled. One sea dog stood on either side of the arched entrance, sneering with suspicion on all who entered.

"Halt! What have we here?" A swarthy arm reached over and made to grab the reins out of Aolwynd's hands. She held onto them all the tighter. Boru secretly touched her leg with his finger. The pirate had jutted out his chin and laid his other hand upon his sword. Aolwynd took the hint and let go.

"Yer' cart's empty, what do it mean?"

The other pirate walked about it looking under the wheels.

She stammered, "My father is already at the market today. We have an inn nearby and we need to buy victuals for our guests."

A gritty smile spread across his face. "Guests? Even now? It must be quite the inn...and when they've eaten their fill I'll warrant you entertain them." His foul breath was so close she could taste the cheese he'd eaten for breakfast. His greasy doublet and leering manner repulsed her but she leaned in close and whispered flirtatiously.

"Aye, I dance for them and sing, but I must get to my father in the market or he will beat me for being late." She made a pout with her lips and sat back.

The pirate let out a dirty chuckle and slapped her thigh leaving his hand there and giving it a friendly squeeze. She took the reins gently from his hands and tried to grin hoping he could not see the fear in her eyes.

Boru stirred beside her. She could feel his hand reaching under his jacket for the dagger she knew he had hidden there.

"And where is this inn? I might needs see this spectacle myself some night."

"Oh, it's a small place, you would find us poor company I fear."

"Where did you say it was?" he snarled, reaching across her lap and grabbing the reins out of her hands once more.

The other pirate was getting impatient. "Oh come on...come on...look at that line! Get on with it! Find her and fuck her in the market later, you're holding everything up!" With that the first devil threw back the reins and slapped the horse's rump. It lurched forward and they were in the city.

Her hands were like ice and her knees shook as they drove through the narrow streets. Aolwynd looked at the gaunt faces of the passersby. On market days the streets used to bustle with activity, not so now. An aura of fear permeated the very walls.

When they pulled into the square it was only half-filled with stalls quickly selling out of the small quantities they had of cheese, vegetables, eggs and milk. A few scrawny chickens clucked pitifully from their wicker cages. The sellers, farmers she had known for years all had a furtive look, cautious, guilty. She sucked in her cheeks as she heard the citizens complaining about raised prices. All were terribly high and there were no bargains, no 'give aways' to family and friends. There were no baker's stalls either with delicious buns, pies and cakes for there was no flour to be had anywhere. Her favorite meat pie man was no where to be seen.

Though the crowd was sparse, it was also desperate. All

were shopping or rather fighting over what little was left to be had. It was well worth the trip for the farmers however, some were even smiling greedily as they took in coin after coin. Not all felt remorse for skinning their customers.

Where before, there would be hearty greetings, gossip between friends and neighbors of marriages and babies, today among the shoppers there was a heavy silence punctuated by grumbling. Everyone got down to business, bought their goods or turned away empty-handed, hurrying from the square. There was no lingering over which wine to buy, for there was no wine, no leisurely making up of minds, no musicians and no comparing prices for everything was dear.

They drove the cart through the square with ease and made their way into the neighborhoods beyond overlooking the harbor.

"Did you see how that pirate watched as we pulled away into the city?" Aolwynd asked.

Boru grunted, but did not answer her, his mind already on the next thing.

They took narrow, quiet streets and approached the harbor in a round about fashion trying not to attract attention and avoid the curious. Sea dogs walked about the streets like kings with whores on their arms or leaned menacingly against the walls of public houses. Aolwynd pulled her cloak about her and stared straight ahead across the horse's rump expecting any moment to be stopped and questioned.

They passed into a neighborhood of houses of the well-to-do. It overlooked the water on a street lined with trees that descended leisurely toward the harbor. Aolwynd turned the cart onto its wide and pleasant prospect. The view of the sea was outstanding but not so now were the homes of the wealthy. Their doors had been flung off their hinges, pillage and destruction lay everywhere. The brigands had taken everything they could carry off and burned the rest or let it drop in the road. Boru had to jump down and remove furniture and other debris as they made their way along the street. Aolwynd hoped that these families had escaped days before. Many were known to her or were friends of her father's.

They followed the sloping street downhill to where the cobblestones ended and out onto a wide wooden promenade. There was a knot of citizens clotted together where the long docks jutted out into the harbor. Their faces were stricken with worry and grief. She pulled the cart up beside them. "Is this where they ransom the prisoners?" she asked.

A woman answered, pulling her shawl tight about her. "Aye, it'll be hours yet, they make the day their own, alreet."

"We've got no choice but stand and wait. You can see them from here, laughing...the devils." another said pointing to one of the ships.

"No use whining, and no use hoping, won't do no good." an old man grumbled.

Boru shifted uneasily in his seat but said nothing.

Aolwynd shivered and looked out to sea as the sun climbed to its highest point in the sky. She shaded her eyes and stared at each ship and thought she saw a boat being lowered to the surface. Yes, there was another boat, and another. Three boats laden with captives and crew came rowing toward the shore. She stood up in the cart impatiently. "I don't see him..."

"Sit down! You draw too much attention to yourself!" Boru growled pulling her by the skirts.

As the boats drew up to the docks she sighed with anguish. Even from a distance she could see the captives

were pitifully thin, ragged, dirty and frightened. Stumbling with their hands tied in front of them, they clambered over the deep sides of the boats and onto dry land. The few women who were among them looked ravaged and stunned. The pirates made free to embrace them and passed them to each other like baggage as they helped them onto the pier. When all were out the victims swayed with sea sickness, stumbling in a sorry herd to stand in line behind a small wooden box. Beside it, ready to begin, sat a pirate with a small table in front of him. His grotesque face was matched only by his demeanor. His eyes were cold, indifferent. His cheek had a red scar and his hair was garish and obviously dyed, blacker than the black leather of his studded jacket. A large gold chain glinted on his neck. He was busy scanning a piece of parchment, drawing one finger down a list of names, his other hand resting on a strongbox.

"I am The Banker!" he called out, rising and stepping up on the box. He stretched his neck to be seen above the crowd. "Here's how it goes! You deal with me and no one else. You don't make no remarks and you keeps your hands in plain sight. When you pays yer ransom you takes yer captive away, quick-like, quiet-like, no squallin', no noise, no nothin'...you just gits! Make yer kisses at home, Ah' doon't wanna see um." The other pirates laughed at his jest. With that he went back to his chair and looking at his list, picked up his quill. "First prisoner! Carolus Arbus!"

The pirates led a gaunt-faced man of about fifty with a bandaged head to the box and prodded him till he stepped up onto it. "Who ransoms this man? Anyone?" A wait of too few moments passed by and he was pulled off the box to one side. His captor whispered in The Banker's ear. "One more week! Next!" The man was shuffled off to the boats as The Banker made a scratch with his pen against his name.

"Junius Melidor!"

This time a man cried out as they half-dragged, half-carried him, lifting him finally upon the box. His eyes were wild, his clothing, of silks and brocades, now hung about him in tatters. He stood with his head swiveling, scanning the crowd.

"Junius Melidor? Anyone?" The Bank called.

No one cried out in answer, 'That's my father!' or 'Uncle! We have found you at last!' The crowd was silent and their faces were turned away from him in shame.

"Right. No time left." The Banker made a gesture across his neck with his quill. A scream came out of the man.

Unconsciously the crowd pulled their coats and shawls about them for protection. Wrenched off the box, he was dragged toward the water. A pirate pushed him down onto his knees and shoved him with his foot till his head hung over the edge of the pier. One of the corsairs took out his sword and with a swift blow, cut off the man's head. It fell into the sea. Then he kicked the body after it.

The crowd moaned.

A woman vomited upon the ground.

Aolwynd could only stare.

"Where is my father?...have we missed him?" she mumbled. Some foolish thought passed through her head that they had been there all along and yet had not seen him paraded right in front of them, instead he had been ignored and dragged off back to the boats.

"Catalina Tricoult!" The Banker shouted.

A young woman in a torn blue gown was displayed next. Her yellow hair was tangled and hung about her face, her bare arms were thin as willow wands and showed bruises where she had been held and forced.

"Anyone?" The Banker said with a grin on his face. "No

family?"

One of the pirates came forward and threw a gold piece on the table. The Banker's hand reached out ever so slowly and palmed it. "Take 'er away."

The young woman kept her eyes lowered as the pirate lifted her up by the waist like a child, her feet dangling and carried her back to the boats.

Aolwynd swallowed hard. "I know that girl." she whimpered, her eyes welling with tears.

"Shhh. Remember what I said." Boru said.

And so it went. Names were called and relatives rushed forward to retrieve their kin. Victims were released, slaughtered or dragged off back to the ships. The sun stretched out her long arms and the sky grew rosy. It was the end of the day and Aolwynd had still not seen her father.

"What are we to do?" she whispered desperately.

"You must go up to The Banker and ask."

Aolwynd gasped. "Please...I can't..."

"Get out of the cart and go up to him. They want money. Have courage." She sat frozen in her seat. Boru pinched her hard on the thigh. Startled, she took a deep breath and climbed down from the cart. Her knees knocked together as she walked through the thinning crowd and approached the table. She touched the pocket of her apron and felt the gold pieces there.

The Banker looked up at her with a scowl. From close up she could see that one eye was clouded over and speckled with red.

"Be gone, wench. We're finished for the day, come back tomorrow."

"Wait, please, my father...Folpas Melior, the spice merchant...The Inn of the Swan, surely you must still have him! He did not come home, he must be here!"

"Maybe he's dead, sweeting? Maybe he fell in a hole in the road."

She gripped the corners of the little table and leaned over him. "Please check your list again, I have gold."

His good eye strayed to her breasts. "Well...let me see..." his hand reached out for hers and pinned it there as he pretended to look down the list, pointing with his other hand at the names. "Nope. No one by that name on my list, my dear."

The other brigands were watching this performance greedily. One of them came close and whispered something in The Banker's ear. He looked up at her. "Well...I'm feeling generous this aft'. Go have a peak in that boat there, there maybe some rubbish in the bottom, see what you will, if it's yer Dah come back and pay me."

Aolwynd's feet flew to the dock. One of the corsairs grabbed her round the waist so she could lean out over the edge and peer into the bottom of his boat. Curled in the shelter of the bow, lying on a heap of ropes was a ragged figure dressed in the filthy remnants of her father's fine clothing. It was Folpas!

"'E was that sick, m'dear, 'E couldn't climb out so we left 'im there. We were going to pitch 'im over the side on the way back. You've saved 'im. Your a good girl, you are." The pirate squeezed her hips before he let her go.

She ran back to The Banker.

"Fifty gold pieces...no...one hundred fer makin' me late t'my dinner. How much 'av you got, eh?" He grabbed her wrist while the others watched. Aolwynd pulled every last coin out of her apron pocket. "There now, that's pretty...that'll do fer yer father, m'lady. Go and claim him." The Banker turned her wrist over still holding it tightly and licked the palm of her hand with his tongue. Aolwynd shuddered and pulled it free. All his companions laughed and hooted.

"Why not keep 'er!" they taunted as she ran away.

"Now, me puppies, we can't have everything we want, can we?" The Banker said watching her go.

Boru wasted no time but gathered the old man up and helped him into the back of the cart.

Taking the reins Aolwynd drove the cart away as soon as they were settled. She felt at any second the devils would let out a yell and come running after them but she looked back and they were unconcerned, too busy loading their prisoners and making ready to cast off. Only The Banker stood at the end of the dock holding his strongbox and staring after her.

Shadows lengthened on the cobbled streets. The only sounds were the rattle of the cart wheels and the clop, clop of the horse's hooves. A chill wind followed them as they left the harbor. Aolwynd shook with the aftermath of fear and excitement, the figure of the girl still caught in her mind. Aolwynd had seen Catalina look up briefly at the sky and back at the city before she was thrown from the arms of one pirate to another and into a boat. Aolwynd began to sob as she drove along and trying to hide her tears. Boru praised her efforts and told her how brave and strong she was but she heard little of it. Only the tone of his voice soothed her once they were away from the sea.

They stopped in a covered passage when they had gotten far enough away to know they were not being followed. Aolwynd climbed into the back and threw her cloak over her father. He was barely alive, yet his eyes were smiling.

"Daughter..." he sighed and fell into unconsciousness.

"Let him rest. Stay with him. I will drive." Boru said.

She hung onto the sides and looked up at the heavens. The streets were empty, taverns were the only bright spots, spilling lamp light and drunken fellows onto the pavement. There seemed to be plenty of drink left in the city for the curbs were decorated with weaving whores and surly types propping them up. They laughed and caroused, strolling about or sat on benches in the open air calling for more ale.

When they returned to the marketplace the square was empty. The horse's hooves echoed loudly against the stone of the houses and the outer wall of the city. It was then that the image of the pirate's girl, her childhood friend, came back again to haunt her. So cold and dark, the place filled her with despair for the girl and her fate. The refuse of the day's market blew about the ground: bits of cabbage leaves and chicken feathers. Broken crockery was piled in a corner but no one was there to clean it up.

"Promise me you will save the city...promise me... Boru." She hesitated for a moment to call him by his given name but he stopped the cart and looked sharp at her, all attention with tenderness in his eyes. "Promise me you will see them all killed or hanged for what they've done."

"My warrior...on my life I promise, if you will follow me..." he whispered then he turned back around and snapped the reins.

They drove on, the end of their adventure lay just ahead.

The great wooden doors of the East Gate were shut when they got to them and the same two pirates sat inside a little guard house drinking. A tavern wench leaned against the outer wall in the shadows, holding an empty jug. She looked at the travelers without much interest. The men stood up slowly and came out with a lamp. The light blinded Aolwynd as it swung in close to her face. It was The Cheese Eater who held it.

"Well now, what's this then? My little friend back again? Praise the sea gods...I was wondering where you'd got to...you didn't leave with the others at close of market, strange to say. Now what's happened, my love? Is this your father then?"

"Doesn't look well a' tall a' tall." said the other pirate leaning into the bed of the cart. "Hard day bargaining?"

Aolwynd stammered. "He's drunk, we're taking him..."

"Doon't even try it lass, we're not so dumb as ye think. E's coom from the harbor en' you've bought 'is freedom, poor ol' basket. An' now you'll 'av ta' do it again..." The lamp revealed his evil grin and the two corsairs exchanged looks.

"Aye! We're ta be paid too, did they no tell ye' tha'?" The pirates laughed nodding to each other.

"I...I gave it all to The Banker. I have nothing more."

"You'll pay up or those doors stay shut! Maybe the old man has something." They looked at Boru but he turned his back to them.

"Eer!" The Cheese Eater said, pursing his lips and winking. "You get down now an' I'll bargain with yah." He grabbed hold of her arm, wrenching her upwards and lifted her out of the cart before she could struggle away. One hand was at her throat in an instant while the other grasped her belt and hustled her into the darkness of the wall.

"Check 'er fer money first!" he said as the other man groped his way from her apron pockets to her bodice and shoved a hand between her legs. She kicked him. "You're a right bitch aren't you?" The Cheese Eater said as he leered into her face and held her still.

The tavern girl gasped and slipped off into the night.

"Ah've been waitin' fer this...hold tha' cart." the pirate said as he pulled her by the belt into a dark corner. "Don't struggle or it'll be the worse fer you." He whispered as his arm went beneath her skirts. His hand reached her thigh, pulling it upward.

Suddenly she heard the other pirate cry out. Boru had

jumped down and was wrestling with him to get the sword out of his hand. He twisted and slammed the man's arm down across his own thigh. The pirate howled and the sword fell to the ground.

Swift as an arrow Boru made for his own blade but the pirate was faster and he pushed Boru against the wheels while retrieving his sword. The jostling cart made her father groan. Boru grabbed hold of the pirate's jacket pulling him so close he could not wield it, then butted him in the head with his own. The man reeled and let go his weapon again, sinking to the ground without a sound. Boru picked up the sword, took a hacking blow to the man's neck and it was done.

While this was happening, The Cheese Eater turned quietly to his partner, dragging Aolwynd further away into a Aolwynd around and pulled her by the belt into the guard house. Boru dove for the door, forcing it open. He stood breathless, staring, sword in hand, his eyes fixed on the pirate's face. "Let her go." he said quietly.

"Doon't come one step nearer or she's for it." The man made a gesture across her throat with his finger and grinned. He rubbed his groin up against her hip to show her he was hard and show Boru he was in control. Aolwynd grimaced with revulsion but took a chance, grabbed his swollen prick beneath his clothing, and twisted with all her might. The Cheese Eater let out a scream and knocked her down.

This was the chance Boru needed. He leapt across the floor of the tiny hut. Aolwynd crawled into a corner but could not keep out of their way as they fought. However, Boru could not swing the sword as there was too little space to do so. He cast it outside the door where it fell into a rain barrel. The pirate immediately came at him and they struggled, rolling and breaking things, flying about the room like trapped birds. Aolwynd was pummeled by their fists and bodies while she watched them, feeling helpless and trying to think. As they turned, the light of the lamp over head shone for a second on Boru's dagger, partially hidden beneath his coat. She reached this way and that snatching at the blade as they circled the room. Finally, Boru had his back to her. She grabbed the pommel of the blade pulling it out and away from their flailing bodies. Hiding it behind her skirts she watched for an opportunity and when it came she sunk it into the The Cheese Eater without pity. He writhed backwards and cried out, arching his neck, his arms reaching out, his mouth open wide. Boru's hands were about the man's throat in an instant and as he sank to the ground he was quickly silenced. Boru crouched over the body making sure he was dead, then retrieved his blade, wiping it off on the pirate's clothing. Boru looked up at her, his chest heaving and wiped his forehead with the back of his hand. A grim smile passed quickly over his face.

"Set this room to rights and put the tankards back on the table. We'll make it look as if they've fallen asleep in their cups and hope no one comes looking till morning."

She stared at him, frozen, her mind blank as a sheet.

"Move!" he barked as he picked up the Cheese Eater's body and set it down on a chair facing the door. He threw a cloak over the corpse's bloody back and rested its head on an arm curled around the tankard.

Then he went out for the other body. Aolwynd tidied the room, trying to avoid the bleeding corpse. She set a lantern

to one side, turning the wick down low so it gave off only a dim light. Boru set the other pirate across from his companion and delicately rested one hand on the man's arm. "There...friend's to the end, an after life too good for either of them."

Leaving the door ajar he helped Aolwynd into the cart then lifted the heavy beam from across the wooden gate and pushed the doors open. Aolwynd drove the cart through and waited on the other side while Boru went back in.

The heavy doors closed and the thump of the beam made her jump. She caught her breath, fearing something, everything, suddenly alone in the dark. Her teeth chattered. The stars seemed cold and the wind blew through her clothing. Looking at her hands she saw they were shaking. She heard a thud as Boru dropped from the wall landing on all fours.

Staring at him, her mouth was set in a pinched line and her eyes wide as an owl's.

"My warrior, are you cold?" Boru took hold of her by the shoulders and rubbed her arms hard. Leaning in he peered cheerfully into her eyes. "It often happens to new recruits, after their first kill...You'll be alright." he said taking the reins.

5

Not a Priest Nor a Jailor

It was midnight when they reached the Inn of the Swan. Against orders to the contrary, Gerda had hung a lamp at the gate. Jorus sat beneath it waiting on a bench. He had been there periodically ever since they left that morning. Boru's men came running from the shadows in every direction as the cart pulled into the courtyard and quickly carried Folpas into the house. Gerda clucked at them all the way up the stairs, fussing and shouting directions.

Boru lifted Aolwynd off the seat. "There's my soldier." he whispered in her ear. As soon as her feet touched the stones she felt the blood leave her head and she dropped, fainting into his arms.

When she awoke, a maid was sitting beside her bed. She raised a candle to Aolwynd's face as the room was dark save for the fire in the hearth.

Laughter came from downstairs.

"How long have I been asleep?"

"Oh, not long, really. You fainted dead away, miss.
Right on them flagstones and Captain Boru, he picked you
up like you was a lark's feather and carried you right into
the house. Right up them stairs he went with you, like he
owned the place and right here in your bed chamber he set
you down!" the maid was dramatic, relishing every word of
her story. "Then...he sat in this very chair and stared at you
for the longest time! What a queer feeling it did give me! I
didn't like to ask him to leave but then the 'Old Harrier'
came in an' I didn't need to, she shooed him out quick
ennuf! Can I get you summit, miss?"

"It's alright...I'm alright...just tired." Aolwynd tried to
recall all that had happened but her mind was too foggy to
sort it out.

"We're that proud of you miss, all of us! Just imagine!
Our mistress... killing pirates!" As soon as the girl said
those words the gorge came up in Aolwynd's throat and she
signaled frantically, her hand across her mouth. The maid
held her steady as she vomited loudly into the chamber pot.

"Oh miss, I'm that sorry!" the maid giggled, struggling
to show her sympathy.

Aolwynd waved her away, staggered over to wash her
face and rinse her mouth with some rosewater from her
dressing table. She donned a green velvet robe over her
shift and tidied her hair, still feeling weak.

The maid dumped the pot out the window. "Here's for
luck! Hope no one's walkin' under it." she laughed.

Another roar came from downstairs.

"Where is everyone?"

"The soldiers are havin' a right good time w'tha pie and
Gerda is mindin' yer father."

"Perhaps that's why they're having a 'right good time'. "

"Aye. They're a bit the worse for wear tonight, they've already finished off yer father's cask of brandy, the one he keeps fer Midwinter Festival."

"And how did they find that?"

"I would be asking Jorus that question, my lady."

Aolwynd tip-toed down the hall to her father's room. The door was ajar and a flickering yellow light cast its beam across the wooden floor. Gerda sat knitting by his bed. She looked up.

"Oh! My bird! You're up? Let me get you something warm..."

"Shhh. Don't fuss. How is father?"

"Just look at him." Gerda pulled aside the heavy bed curtain. "It's terrible what they done to him, see how dreadful thin he is."

Folpas looked pale and small in his big bed, his nightshirt swam about him and the open collar spread out like two white wings showing the cords in his neck and his breastbone prominent.

"You sit here whilst I go down and tell those ruffians to be quiet!" Gerda announced.

"No!" whistled a reedy voice from the bed. "Let them enjoy themselves, we have much to thank them for..."

"Father!" Aolwynd cried and though she wanted to fall on him and weep aloud, she caught her breath and slowly, carefully sat down upon the counterpane taking his pro-offered hand.

"How did I get here? You must tell me everything..." he wheezed. It took all his breath just to say these few words.

"Hush, it can wait till morning."

"Gerda told me....You...that captain...dangerous...I daren't remember." he shook his head at her as if she were a child.

"Gerda lies." she smiled. "Please rest." Aolwynd rose and went to the door catching the old woman's eye. "I will come back and take over for you."

Gerda wiped Folpas' forehead with a wet cloth and waved her away. "You go back to bed, that's what you do."

Aolwynd meant to do as she was told but the noise and laughter drew her downstairs. 'I will just look in and thank them.' she thought as she teetered down the stairs holding onto the bannister.

A fire blazed brightly in the kitchen hearth, candles burned everywhere. On chairs and benches about the room and near the fire soldiers were joking and plying their captain for a detailed report of the rescue. The serving girls were mincing about, flirting and refilling any cup that was hoisted into the air. On the table, the remains of a glorious feast, in the center of which stood the remains of the veal pie, all but devoured. Golden crusts lay crumbled about the floor with insignificant morsels of cheese being finished by the dogs.

Glad to see them enjoying themselves, she stood watching silently. The celebration reassured her and she let those images of violence and despair that had been seeping into her consciousness retreat again.

Suddenly all the men grew silent and their eyes turned on her. A great roar came out of them, they sprang to their feet and crashed their cups together. "A toast! A toast to our Swan!"

Boru stood up. He had gotten rid of the gardener's clothing and was again his handsome self. He took her hand and raised his cup. "My Shadow." he whispered, drained it and threw it into the fire. His men roared again and called for more drink.

Laughter and singing followed them across the hall and faded away as he closed the study door. His breath smelled of brandy and his hands were warm as he slid them up her arms to her neck. Swaying a little with drink he cradled her head in his palms and kissed her. His lips were dry and insistent as if he were dying of thirst and her mouth was the spring from which he drank. His arms wrapped about her. Lifting her up he carried her to the fireplace laying her down upon the hearth stone. The slate was warm against her back and she reveled in the feeling. Letting it course through her sore muscles she lifted her arms and closed her eyes.

He had made love before, first to his father's mistress who had taught him how to please a woman, then to the countless and faceless wenches and serving girls of his two campaigns. These were women to joke about afterwards with the men around the campfire. But this was different, she was different. He was beginning to feel for her a love almost like family, no, closer than family, for he burned with desire for her, 'How could this be like family?' he thought as his confident grin slipped away from his face. 'A bride?', he thought.

She knew they were one that night as they were always meant to be.

Their ardor consumed them until near dawn, when, as they lay in each other's arms the embers of the fire broke and rolled onto the hearth reminding them that a bed was waiting on the floor above. They climbed the stairs to her chamber, not caring who might see them, disheveled and dragging their clothes behind them. Whispering, giggling and shushing each other like naughty children they locked the door to her room. Then, as lovers they rocked the bed before, at last, they fell asleep.

Late in the morning Gerda came pounding at the door.

Boru sprang out of bed and hopped about first on one leg then the other as he struggled to put on his breeches and boots. Aolwynd stifled a laugh as he pranced about. Throwing her a kiss he grabbed his shirt and jacket and climbed out the window. She ran to the ledge just in time to see him drop to the ground like a cat.

"Coward!" she called after him. He grinned widely and waved his shirt at her as he headed to the sleeping hall.

Aolwynd looked about the room and sighed. She kicked a pillow aimlessly out of the way and opened the door.

"Are you ill? Why did you lock the door?" Gerda asked, surveying the damage.

"How is father?"

"Sleeping. Why was your door locked?"

Gerda passed by her, approaching the bed as if it were some kind of crouching animal, lying in wait.

"I...did not sleep well last night. Bad dreams."

Gerda picked up a pillow and pulling the covers from the bed with a flourish she stared at the sullied and torn sheets. "Must have been some nightmare." She wrinkled her nose.

Aolwynd snapped at her. "You're not my priest nor my jailer! I'm a grown woman and the mistress of this house I'll have you remember! I've made my choice, as if you couldn't guess, given him my heart...and there's an end to it!"

Instead of shouting, Gerda put her hand to her forehead and turned away. "Your heart and everything else...Oh...we'll never see you married now...blast them soldiers...I knew no good would come of running an inn..." the old woman moaned softly with sadness in her voice.

Aolwynd came up behind her and placed her chin on one boney shoulder, pressing down as they used to do till one or the other of them would flinch away, ticklish. Gerda did not react. Aolwynd held her about the waist. "Please, Sweeting, don't cry. Only mother I have ever known, try to understand. He is good, he is noble, he will not fail me."

The old woman turned then and looked at her with the eyes of a hawk. Aolwynd knew she was about to get a dose of truth whether she was ready or not.

"Fail you? That is exactly what he will do...he'll never marry you, for he's not allowed to. You're right, he's noble...and you're not."

Aolwynd turned her face away.

"His father will forbid it, if your 'princeling' even goes so far as to tell him. The Guardians marry girls from the highest families in Earden. They make blood bargains with their children like breeder stock at the market."

"But his own mother is from our city."

"She was high born, from a very old house. You are a merchant's daughter, nothing more...and now something less than that. Thanks to the pirates your wealth is gone...and you run an inn, remember? Lower in station than you ever were before! I had hoped to marry you into one of our own ancient houses but when you began to take coin...and now...after last night..." she glanced at the bed and sucked her teeth. "deflowered and penniless." She sighed bitterly. "Neither use nor ornament, as my mother would say. Worthless." Gerda added softly "No more now than a soldier's whore."

Aolwynd whirled around. "Enough! How dare you say that to me!"

"What do you think? That he's never had a woman before? Never supped at that particular cup? And you so graciously laid out for him all your delights!" Gerda made a sweeping gesture with her hand toward the bed. "Sweet as you are, and on my life, as I love you...you are only one of hundreds who've opened their legs to him, in haylofts, on kitchen tables, on the floor, I'll warrant, only one of many he has had, has had and left behind."

"Go away! Never speak to me of this again, no matter what happens, for good or for ill, he's mine, I've made my choice. He's mine."

"Oh, but that's just it, my dove...he isn't yours." Gerda 'drove in the knife' as her father would have said. She threw her arms about Aolwynd and they clung to each other for a moment.

Aolwynd was the first to let go. "Stop fussing." she said coldly, straightening her shoulders and closing the subject. "I want my breakfast and a wash. Have one of the maids bring me hot water. I'm in no mood for any more talk. Yes, and clean sheets for our bed."

Gerda looked up at this but left the room without correcting her.

6

Clumsy Poetry

From the bliss of the night, Aolwynd now fell into a murderous depression as if she were thirteen years old all over again. She paced about her room and for a time she blamed it all on Gerda's spiteful words. She picked up a mirror from her dressing table and looked at her face. The woman she saw there had a lover. Now the angry eyes of her childhood spent waiting for him looked back at her. She threw the looking glass across the room breaking it into pieces. She sat at her table till her mind let go of its burden and her thoughts drifted away on a shaft of afternoon light.

Suddenly voices and commotion came from the stable yard. The clatter of hooves awoke her from her lethargy. She shuffled to the window and saw Boru and three others take the road east.

She ran down the stairs in her shift but Gerda called her a strumpet and held her back out of sight.

A scout had come from the approaching army and Boru had ridden out to greet them.

Ah! The blue cloud of loneliness that surrounded her then! Miserable, she dressed without care, still aching for his body and his touch, unwilling to let those sensations go. Every cinch of her belt buckle made her recall his hands about her waist, the feel of her blouse against her breast made her thrill.

She tried to avoid everyone in the household by staying upstairs and tending to her father. Slowly, lost in fussing over him she tamed these new feelings and her longing faded. Yet as she sat while Folpas slept she marveled that people could make love and then simply go about their lives, cook dinner, ride a horse, fight a battle. Wouldn't everything remind one of their lover's touch? Wouldn't everything, every word, even a name, generate a sigh? She had stepped out of an intimate world into the vast and totally uninteresting landscape of the everyday. 'This is torture.' she thought with a smile.

The sun went down and came up again before there was any sign of Boru's return. Toward noon the sound of thousands of marching feet was heard reverberating through the hills. An army, dozens of companies, boiled over the crest of the road, their shields bearing the green maze or the spiral, emblems of their various units. Boru rode at their head and beside him, in battle gear much like his own, rode an even younger boy. Boru stretched out his arm signaling to the host. The companies fell out and began to make camp on the wide plain across from the inn, just below the crest, out of sight of the city.

Aolwynd watched with fascination, their tents and

cooking fires springing up almost like magic. She spied the many camp followers amongst them, women setting up their homes, getting out their cooking pots, their children whooping down the aisles between the tents.

Boru and two other riders came on to the inn.

Aolwynd rushed from her father's window to her chamber, threw gowns about the floor, found a pretty one of rose brocade and fidgeted while a girl coiffed her hair. She ran down the stairs to the courtyard and would have flung her arms about his neck as he leapt down from his horse but he shook his head ever so slightly in warning and addressed her formally. Stunned, she caught her breath and recovered her dignity enough to drop him a curtsey.

He bowed and nodded with a face like a dancing master whose student has remembered a difficult step. "Lady Aolwynd, may I present my brother, Faolan, of the House of the Supreme Guardian, and our Councilor General, Halduro."

"Ah!" said the older man. "A lady running an inn? This I have never seen, though I have heard of this place. A safe inn for travelers, I hear, and now I see why. Boru told me of your bravery, you must be a formidable opponent! I will be sure to pay my bill!" He looked about in vain for appreciation of his joke.

"I am a daughter of Saels, I will help my city and you anyway I can." Aolwynd replied stiffly. Boru stood off to the side looking amused.

Faolan was tongue-tied as any youth might be encountering a beautiful woman just a little older than himself. He stared openly at her breasts, then shyly smiled and realizing his discourtesy, looked away, affecting a proud, manly indifference which melted into childish excitement as he gazed about him. His hair was fair, like his brother's and cut to hang just above the shoulders like his. In fact his walk was so like Boru's that Aolwynd thought he might be making fun of him. She almost laughed till she realized he mimicked him out of love for the man. The sweetness of this touched her heart. Faolan bowed formally to her and placed one hand on his chest as he swept the other gesturing forward that she might walk ahead of them.

"He would follow you into the lands of the dead." she whispered to Boru as they climbed the steps into the house.

"That is truth," he said "and I would die to protect the puppy. This is his first campaign, can you tell?"

"Don't be mean."

"Aye, and by the look of things you're already on his side. You'll be his first campaign as well. Forewarned is forearmed." Boru's arm curled about her waist then, he slowed down so that they were left alone beneath the shadows of the staircase. "How fares my lady today and how is your good father?" He kissed her sweetly, not waiting for an answer.

"Better now you show me some affection." she pouted.

"Patience, my flower. I have a city to re-take, my mind is on that business. But I will not neglect you, while I may. And your father?"

"He is resting. It will be a slow recovery, he is very weak."

"I would visit him when you think he is strong enough."

They walked arm in arm toward the back of the inn and entered a long dining hall, descending two steps and pausing beneath an archway. The great table was surrounded by his officers eating and drinking. Sheafs of wheat decorated the walls, sconces and torches illuminated the diners. Fresh rushes had been spread across the floor that gave off a green and pleasant scent as they were stepped upon. A fire roared in the fireplace at the end of the hall and her hounds lay in front of it gnawing bones contentedly.

The table was laden with all good things, roasted birds, hams, pies and a platter of sweet meats. Bowls of cooked vegetables, jugs of gravy accompanied all. Breads, cheeses and cakes stood waiting on a side board with a cask of mead. Gerda had got the place up like it was Mid-Winter Festival.

Indeed, the arrival of the troops had everyone in the house singing as if the battle were already over. The maids were in a tizzy, not knowing which of the handsome officers to flirt with first. Jorus sat by the fire on a little stool strumming his lute.

"What is all this?" Aolwynd whispered into Gerda's ear as the old woman sampled the scrapings from the bottom of a roasting pan.

"Your father would have it so. He would thank them for their service to this house." She cast an evil look in Boru's direction as he came up to them.

"I need no thanks," he said squeezing Aolwynd's waist discreetly with his hand. "I have all I desire."

"Have you? I am glad, I thought..." Aolwynd cleared her throat and changed the subject. "In the city, I was so frightened, all my strength came from you."

"You are stronger than you know."

She kissed him on the cheek and he looked about the room in embarrassment. He left her company then and joined his officers. Aolwynd stared after him, confused again. Clearly there were many things about men she did not understand. Turning her attention toward the things she had command of, she marched through to the larder muttering to herself. She was curious to see if Gerda had left anything to eat or was every last morsel of food on the dining boards in the hall for 'those men' to devour.

Walking back through the house, she noticed a light coming from her father's study. She found Faolan perusing the shelves, touching the leather scroll boxes and reading the titles aloud to himself.

"Feel free to borrow what you will, my lord."

He jumped back, his cheeks flushing, but recovered himself quickly. "I did not mean to intrude..." he stammered, "it's just that I am so fond of history and I was drawn in. Your father has such a collection, we have not the match of it in all of Guardia I think, even among the great libraries."

"That is a sweet compliment, I will tell my father. He is a scholar as was his father before him. Men came from far and wide to spend time arguing with him, or so it seemed to me." She smiled, leaning against the work table and watched the youth as his fingers passed over the shelves.

"Oh but I thought your father was a tradesman?"

"A merchant, yes, but he rides more than one horse...as could you, if you had a mind to."

Faolan blushed and came close to her, running his fingers over the leather covering of the table following the gold embossing along its edge. "My father wants only soldiers. Those who obey his orders fare best."

"And you? What do you want?"

"You see through me right away...Lady...Aolwynd?"

"Yes."

"Aolwynd. How beautiful." He turned away and took a scroll down from the shelf unrolling it as far as the table would allow. It was a compendium of all the beasts of the known world, even beyond the shores of Earden. The creatures were carefully painted to show their features and written beneath each one was its particular attributes. Aolwynd had not seen this scroll for a long time, it had been her favorite as a child. She pointed out the brightly-colored birds. They bent over each picture losing themselves in the pleasure of discovery. Faolan leaned in so close to her that his cheek almost touched hers. He took a strand of her hair that had fallen loose and tucked it behind her ear.

Aolwynd jerked back. "I think we should re-join the others. Are you not hungry, my lord?"

"There are other things to hunger for besides food." he breathed, looking deeply, seriously into her eyes.

She flashed him a smile, trying not to laugh. "Come, take my arm, you may escort me to the dining hall."

The youth took her hint and standing only a little taller than herself, they made a handsome couple as they entered. He held her arm with exaggerated courtesy until she was seated at the head of a table then sat down next to her where there was already a plate of food and a goblet of wine.

"Oh no, little brother...That is my place, not yours." Boru said pulling him up by the collar, smiling at Aolwynd all the while.

Faolan grimaced and moved to another place.

The hall was getting warm and so were the men. They laughed and loosened their belts, called for more mead or wine and bussed the serving girls.

After what seemed like a goodly amount of time Aolwynd made her regrets and bade them all goodnight. They paid little attention to her so busy were they with singing and urging Jorus to play one tune after another. Faolan had fallen asleep by his plate, his head resting upon his arm.

Aolwynd climbed the stairs and went to sit with her father. She could hear horses clattering in and out of the courtyard. It was hard to tell anymore what was happening that might demand her attention. All was chaos and military busyness. The noise and the many comings and goings made for an exciting confusion. She felt proud that the siege of the city was being planned from her inn. It was '...one thing to read history, another to live it!' she remembered her father's words.

He was sleeping, or so it appeared. As she tip-toed into the small circle of candlelight she saw Boru sitting quietly beside the bed.

"I'm standing watch for one of your maids so she might get a bite to eat."

Aolwynd nodded. "Thank you sir, you are ever courteous."

Those cold eyes of his momentarily returned. "My lady." he said softly.

"Who is there?" came her father's reedy voice.

"Oh...we have woken you!" Aolwynd whispered, bending over and kissing his damp forehead.

"No, I was awake. My lord? I must thank you...Aolwynd, help me to sit up."

"No! Stay! Do not trouble yourself." Boru smiled and held the old man down upon his bed till he relaxed and lay back against his pillows. "You will not think us so welcome when we have cleared out your larder and emptied your cellars of drink."

"You are welcome to all I have...of my goods." he said softly with a glance toward his daughter. "You have given me back what is most precious to me. Without offending my guest...may I speak with my daughter alone?"

"Of course." Boru bowed immediately and left the room.

"Daughter."

Aolwynd turned away from her father and began pouring a glass of wine for him diluted with water.

"I would caution you."

"Please, father."

He sighed. "Gerda has told me."

"She talks too much."

"I fear you will be hurt. Now listen. This captain is a fine young officer, but more than that, he may rule the country some day. Think on it. He is like the mountain eagles we see in the spring, far above us, circling, only coming down into the valley when the new lambs are there. They feed on the young that stray, but they mate only with eagles."

Aolwynd rolled her eyes derisively and opened her mouth to protest.

"I know, I know...forgive your old father his clumsy poetry, I am a scholar not a poet. But it is nonetheless true." He held up a shaking hand. "I see the love in your eyes. I see you so full of life, a fine woman you have grown up to be. Strong and willful, yes, like your mother, but you've kept your sweetness as she did. No wonder he is drawn to you. I am proud. Whatever happens...and he is a good man....I see that. What ever happens, your home is here, you need never be ashamed or fear the future. But remember, his duty is to Earden, and to his father, and he will not forget to do it. The Guardians do not turn away from their duties."

Aolwynd bit her lip till she was out of Folpas' sight, slowly nodding her head as she backed away from his bed. She fled his room in tears. Bumping into the maid on her return she shot her a look that would curdle new milk.

She went to her chamber and locked the door. Leaning against its solid planks she wept at the truth of her father's words. They were not words she cared to hear.

The room was dark save for the red coals of the fireplace. Sparks flew as a log was thrown on top of them. Boru sat in her chair warming his hands. She wiped her eyes and looked at him solemnly.

"Your father was very eloquent. Forgive me for listening near the door. You're right not to trust me. Why should you? I'm a plain soldier, fit for battle, we march and we move on. That has been my life so far. Warriors were ever unkind to those they love. You've seen the women and children who follow us. It is hard. What life would that be for a lady like yourself? And he's right. I have the burden of my house. My father is adamant and getting worse as he grows old. Though I love him, I say it, he is cold and demanding. I am never happier than when I am away from Guardia, gone on some errantry."

She crept nearer to him and sat on a cushion by the hearth. "Are there many fine ladies at court?"

Boru smirked. "Of course." He'd heard that question many times before.

"Are there any that you...might wed?"

"A few. But I hate court life. I cannot abide the simpering and the gossip...the scheming. My father revels in it and is good at turning the wheel in his favor. Not I. I itch to get away again as soon as I am home. They're all alike, those creatures, cut from the same damask cloth they go on about. And the men...their minds are like mill stones. I hear the wheels grinding out their schemes even before they speak. They cannot be trusted." He took her hand and bent it down absent-mindedly. "Give me a warrior. You're not like them. It's why I love you...yes, I love you. I cannot picture any of them doing what you have done. But what to do with you...that is what I do not know." He bent over and threw another log on the fire.

"Then we must wait until we know." Aolwynd said.

"Now, my little lamb...before I fly away," he said as he lifted her up in his arms.

Again he was gone by morning, nor did he wake her.

She heard no horses, no men at arms in the yard. Her mind was full of the night before. It spun in a small circle that revolved around the touch and smell and warm force of his embrace. When she finally tore herself away from the spell of remembrance, she threw off the covers, washed, dressed in a gown of blue linen and went downstairs.

It was late morning. The air was chill, the sky cloudy and the dew hard that clung to the ivy on the north wall. Winter was approaching. All her fine soldiers had gone. The sleeping hall was empty, their pallets stacked, showing the naked ropes and boards. The fireplace still smoldered with coals.

Her hounds found her sitting there and padded about the sleeping hall aimlessly snuffing the floor for scraps of food left behind, any remnant. She felt like them.

7

The Twin Gods of War

As she walked back toward the house she heard a horse enter the gate. It was a single rider. Faolan dismounted and holding the reins walked toward her with a smile.

"I've come to look in your library again, if it please you."

"Aren't you preparing for battle?"

"We've just arrived! You will find, my lady, that an army moves along just as slowly as a tinker's cart..." Faolan remarked importantly, puffing out his chest. "many things must be sorted out before we lay siege to such a great city. And not battle, unless they come forth, which they won't...the cowards, they'll stay inside the walls. They are not soldiers." Obviously parroting what he had heard, her amused look made him relax, his boyish grin returned.

"Anyway, I doubt the war councils will include me." He gazed through the gate toward the tents and banners.

"Why do you say that?"

He sighed. "If I were not The Supreme Guardian's son I would never have been allowed in the first one. I'd be no more than a squire and only that for many a year. As it is I wear the armor but do not deserve it."

"I wish I were a man." she mumbled.

"Don't wish that." he said touching her sleeve.

"Why not? To see the world, meet strange peoples, wield a sword...how is that not better than what I am?"

"I hear you are not bad with a dagger. A woman to be reckoned with. Besides, there are other things, more important."

"Keeping house? Children?" she scoffed. "Duties my nurse used to drum into me till she saw I was deaf to them. I know now I was right."

"Ah. Your rescue of your father. I was told your knees were knocking." he teased.

"Yes...he told you that? But now I think on it, I remember the excitement, the test of it. Not knowing from second to second what would happen and rising to meet the challenge, oh horrible, yes...but thrilling too. Being in the moment and only the moment...using your wits and changing your fate!"

Faolan hung on her words. "I have yet to see battle. This is the first time father has let me go and still he sends Halduro to watch over me! I don't need a wet nurse!"

"Of course not."

He seemed to stand taller because of her confidence in him. He smiled. "I see we have much in common."

"Yes, we both have jailers..." Gerda was peering out at them from her kitchen window.

"Would you like to see the encampment?"

Aolwynd's heart leapt in her breast. "Would it be alright, do you think?"

"We'll never be noticed. They pay no attention to me. They're making siege towers, would you like to see them?"

He jumped onto his horse. She climbed onto a bench and he pulled her up behind him. Putting her arm about his waist, she grasped the worn leather cantle of the saddle behind her with the other hand. Faolan rested his forearm on hers and they rode sedately out like a picture in one of her father's scrolls.

She'd never seen so many men, horses, tents, banners in one place. It was a moveable city with rows of little streets laid out across the field. People were coming and going with armor,
weapons, buckets and food. She was fascinated by the women who seemed right at home doing their chores, cooking, washing clothes. Would she feel at home amongst them? Yelling for her brats? Carrying away the slop bucket every morning? Would she be praying with the other women to the pyre of flames consuming effigies of the Twin Gods of War? Would Boru wish this life for her? And if they did not marry, would she have a place here, amongst 'honest' women? His mistress not his wife, half fish and half fowl. No place in the palace, no place in camp. Shunned. Was this what he had in mind when he said he did not know what to do with her? Did she wish this or any of this for herself?

She clung to Faolan's waist, shifting back and forth with the leisurely gait of his mount. He clearly enjoyed being her guide, pointing out the smithy at his forge, the smoke rising, swords and armor stacked in piles about him. They passed the lines of war horses, their enormous flanks shining in the sun. He rode by particular tents, their banners and shields mounted outside. These were the men he most admired. Lastly, his brother's tent with its round shield suspended on a post. She looked about furtively, hoping not to be seen, but they were lost in the crowd and rode on with confidence to a wide trampled field surrounded by pine forest.

Men were cutting down trees and shaping them into logs. At the road side, tall siege towers were being built and also storming ladders. Faolan found a spot under an oak and they dis-mounted. They sat and talked of their childhoods, sharing stories. Close to his brother, she felt she understood a little more of Boru's past and his life as a noble. Of his duties.

As the sun fell in the west, Halduro came upon them. He reined in his horse at some little distance and waved for Faolan to mount and join him. Aolwynd could not hear what was being said but the youth looked increasingly angry and embarrassed, his cheeks burning. Suddenly he jerked the reins of his horse about and galloped off.

She was left standing alone.

Halduro rode up to her slowly. He had a grim look on his face as he gazed down at her. "Your place is at the inn...my lady." These last words came out with such exaggerated emphasis that she knew he meant to call her something very different, if he dared. There was poison in his next utterance. "Boru is a man and may do as he likes with whomever he will, but Faolan is my charge. I do not wish him soiled with your company. Go back to your place." He did not wait to see her reaction, nor hear any word of protest but simply turned his horse and rode away.

Aolwynd's cheeks flushed and her mouth dropped open. Anger and shame mingled together with indignation in her breast. She looked about her with tears in her eyes. This man sat at my father's table only the night before. He praised me when we met. Was this the courtly courtesy

Boru spoke so bitterly about, she thought.

Gerda's words came back to her as she scrambled through the blackberry bushes and out onto the road. The thorns in the brambles cut her arms and ripped at her skirts. She pulled at them in a fury and her apron tangled there, impossible to free. With a wrench she took it off and left it hanging.

'Am I a soldier's whore? Is that what the world thinks of me? Not Faolan, surely not Boru, but yes, the rest of my world, the maids, even Gerda. The soldiers...my beloved soldiers, surely they still thought of me as their own little Swan. And what of father...' his words came back to her also. Yes, they were already resigned to it. It was she who had just caught up with them. 'Because of this simple act of love, to give one's body, a gift exchanged between two lovers...was I not free in this world to give of myself and receive his love in return?' Her thoughts tortured her all the way home but she knew the answer to them. Everything in this world has a price. He was no ordinary person...one of importance. He was free to love, but not to commit.

Her face was smudged with tears and her mind worn out from nonsense, excuses and explanations by the time she reached the inn. The dust of the road marred her shoes and the hem of her gown was caked with dirt. Little beads of blood punctuated the scratches on her arms and legs.

The kitchen was noisy with preparations for supper. She collapsed on a bench outside and put her head in her hands. She looked without feeling at the empty courtyard. The pear tree was naked, its fruit all gone. Dry leaves skittered across the paving stones.

So many years of waiting, the dream of him, the touch of his hands, her body so willing to take him in, to possess him, to feel him possessing her. But that was as far as it went. She owned nothing of him. To think about it anymore made her head pound. She felt the cold wind blow and saw the warm light from the kitchen window beckoning. She knew Gerda's arms would be there to comfort her, but she would not seek them any more than she could go back to being an innocent child.

Instead she walked slowly up to her room. The nails of her hounds clattered up the stairs behind her. She paid no heed to Gerda's worried calls. Aolwynd held the door open for her dogs then closed and bolted it.

This time she was alone.

'What do I possess?' This question harried her all night. She had been named a whore by someone she did not respect, but some one she did respect had said she was 'stronger' than she knew. What did she have that was her own? What did she call herself?

By daybreak she had the answer.

"It's time to reopen the inn." she told the household as they gawped at her over their porridge.

Gerda smiled. "And where was your captain last night?"

Aolwynd was coy and banked down her anger as she'd been taught. "Perhaps he found some other occupation?"

"Or some other woman, I'll warrant...just as well."

"What do you mean by that?" Aolwynd flared up. The servants hurriedly finished their breakfast and began to leave the table casting looks at each other. They'd seen pots fly before. "Look out in that field! There are thousands of soldiers out there, or are you blind? There is a city full of starving, terrified people. He's meant to be doing something about that, isn't he?"

Gerda shrugged.

Aolwynd did not feel like defending him but neither did she feel like wasting any more tears, nor sitting down at the kitchen table and pouring out her sorrows to all and sundry over their milk toast and porridge. Nor...would she be telling them about Halduro and his cruel remarks.

"I will need Jorus, his boy and a couple of maids this morning, we are going to put the courtyard to rights as it was before the soldiers got here, and tell the maids to set up the dining hall for winter use."

Gerda opened her mouth to protest but shut it again. She knew it was futile to resist any project her mistress sunk her teeth into.

"Have the girls remove anything of our family from the entry hall, anything we do not want damaged or stolen. This is a public house again. Then surround the great table with smaller ones, chairs or benches for each. Is father's tray ready? I will take it up." With that Aolwynd swept out of the room with her nose in the air, broaching no disagreement. The kitchen cat followed after her with its tail waving like a flag.

Gerda let out a laugh like a bark as she scrubbed a pot. "There they go, the queen of dishrags and her court!" For all her complaints there was something of pride and relief in her voice.

They cleaned the leaves out of the flowerbeds and set up tables and benches. The air was still warm in the day time and she needed to have things look the way it had before, if only for her own sake. Jorus pried up some paving stones and dug a great fire pit. He was told to kill a pig and roast it on a spit right there in the courtyard. If there were any travelers within ten miles they would smell it. She pulled out the tavern sign he had carved for her so long ago, the one Folpas said they would never need and together with Jorus' boy they hung it just outside the gate. It was a white swan gliding across a field of blue. No one could mistake its meaning, but to Aolwynd it was like her shield and she was getting ready to fight her own battle with it.

The smell of roast pork filled the air with a delicious

fatty smoke that wafted out over the fields. They soon had several visitors. Farmers coming back from the city stopped in for a tankard of ale. They knew Folpas and were glad to hear of his rescue and recovery. They were also full of gossip. She did not tell them much of her own adventure or correct their stories, no one needed to find a connection between her father's rescue and the death of the two pirates. Instead she took the opportunity to buy what was left of their produce and arrange for them to come first to her on their way to market. It was a happy meeting for all.

The news from the city was grim. More ships had been seen coming from the south and rumors of an alliance with murderous tribes had also been heard. The pirates had put to death any lingering hostages and were looking for new victims. The market was a feeble and desperate place now where only the lowliest of servants went from houses that could still afford to buy goods. Expendable. A rumor there was that the pirates would soon bar all the gates and let the people starve, then send threats to the Supreme Guardian of Earden, ransoming the whole city.

The streets were not safe at night since the slaying at the Eastern Gate and the sea dogs had doubled their guard keeping track now of everyone who entered or left the city. They questioned all who passed through concerning the slaying and if one could believe it, they were meaner and uglier than before. They were even offering gold for any information leading to a capture.

Aolwynd thought of the tavern maid who had run off into the night, part of her wished the girl dead. "Did they ever find out who killed those corsairs?"

"Not yet." one farmer said.

She thanked them all before they left and asked if they would spread word that her inn was open for business.

As the sun went down a few soldiers came, lured by the

smell of roast pig. They sat around tables outside till it was too cold then went in reluctantly, begging Jorus to bring the meat. He and a soldier carried the glistening body on its stave into the dining hall and slammed it down on a side board. Jorus was carving plates of pork as quickly as he was able. The serving maids dished out boiled cabbage, pots of mustard, dark bread and slabs of butter. Ale flowed as fast as the maids could pour it. Gerda sat at her table in the kitchen grinning like a tax collector counting the money.

The soldiers did not stay long however, they fed themselves and slipped back to camp. As they left, the officers began to wander in. Aolwynd laughed to see the coins piling up, at least she could have revenge on Halduro by luring his troops away from their fires. It was petty of her but it made her smile.

She moved about the hall, chatting with those she knew, refilling their cups and asking about their families. This was her realm, her kingdom. She ruled here. In the doorway she spied Faolan standing, his gaze adjusting to the darkness and smoke of the room. Their eyes met and she bade him come sit by the fire and brought him a plate of food. He bowed and handed her the apron without a word. His guilty expression, said everything.

In strode Halduro and seeing Faolan he pushed his way through the men toward the hearth.

"I told you not to come here!" he spat, taking the plate out of the youth's hands and throwing it into the flames.

"Leave my house, sir, only my guests are welcome here and you are no longer one of them." Aolwynd came over to them.

Halduro turned and glared at her.

Faolan rose. "The lady asks you to leave, general." His voice shook and broke but his eyes were black.

"This...you call a lady?" Halduro hissed too low for the other men to hear. "Your mother was a lady...not this. Come with me now."

Aolwynd stepped back and saw Boru behind Halduro. As Halduro reached out to grab Faolan by the arm, Boru did the same to him and spun him around.

"What are you doing?"

"Protecting my charge."

"From what?"

"From unhealthy influence..." Halduro said staring at Aolwynd.

"From pork and cabbage, captain." she said.

Halduro winced at her joke and turned as if by habit, whipping the back of his hand around to strike. Faolan jumped in front of her and took the blow.

Boru pulled out his sword.

A great clatter of chairs falling over and scraping of benches followed as everyone in the room backed away from their tables.

"Do not ever lay your hands on my brother again." Boru growled, the point of his sword an inch away from Halduro's throat. Boru spoke to the youth without taking his eyes from the general. "What's going on?"

"I came to bring back our lady's apron. She dropped it yesterday."

Boru's eyebrow raised but he said nothing.

"Get out!" Boru backed away, waving his sword and giving Halduro room to move. "We will talk more of this later."

Halduro raised his hands palms out in mock surrender and bowed. His eyes sought Aolwynd's as he left the hall. They were full of vengeance, hers were cold.

The hounds made short work of the burnt food on the hearth, pawing at the fiery bits and running off with the bones. The men returned to their tables. There was much grumbling and agreement amongst them, he was not well liked, this general.

Two plates and tankards were brought to the brothers and they sat, eating together by the fire. Faolan told of the visit to the siege towers. Aolwynd took away their empty plates and he told his brother the rest when she had gone.

She was back with a poppyseed cake for Faolan and he joined the officers rolling dice.

"I am sorry you had to walk back unescorted, that was grave discourtesy, we will not let that happen again, not to 'Our Lady'." Boru emphasized the phrase. "I warned you about that puppy. He had so little time with our lady mother, he will moon over you until you are sick of him."

"He's a fine man, or will be some day. He has you to thank for that, I think."

Boru shrugged his shoulders but smiled proudly. "I'm glad you have re-opened the inn. It can serve us still."

"It serves me well enough."

"You can keep your ears open for me."

"Of course." She told him all she had heard from the farmers. He listened, his lips closed in a grim line.

"Be careful whom you serve here, and watch your maids, don't let them talk."

"Then I will have to gag them, or lock them in the larder."

Looking about the room, they watched one girl leaning over the dice game, distracting the players with her charms and another brazenly sitting on an officer's lap.

"Hmmm. I see what you mean. I don't suppose you would care to sit on my lap?"

"I might like to if we were alone, but as I have already lost my good name, I have little left but the pretense of one in company."

Boru took her hand and glowered into the fire.

The night wore on and the officers left taking Faolan with them. Boru stayed by the fire. She kissed his temple and went to the kitchen to see about tomorrow's menu and to see what had been earned, then she stepped outside for air.

All was black save the coals of the roasting pit still glowing. Someone was poking them and making them spark. She thought it was Jorus and went over to thank him.

It was Halduro.

"You are not welcome here, my lord." Aolwynd spoke boldly and turned to go.

He grabbed her arm. "Some say you are brave but I call you a brazen little whore and dangerous." He turned her round putting his arm about her neck and tightening it while he held her other arm against her back. "I could have you killed and no one would be the wiser. I would do it myself but I would not want soiled blood on my blade."

"You insult me and yet you sat at my father's table!" she cried out as she struggled to get free.

"Listen to it! She's insulted? You and your city, little better than the pirate scum that took you. Blood mixed for generations with the very dogs that sit in your harbor! That's all you are and now we have to defend you?" he whispered in her ear, "Even their mother was little better than you...noble?" He spat on the ground."What if I take you into the bushes right now? You've been there before, I'll warrant. That would turn my boys against you! Shall I make you howl like the bitch you are?"

"Let her go!" Jorus yelled running around the corner of the house, but Boru was quicker.

Halduro pushed her into Jorus arms and drew his weapon. "Come, my boy...she's not worth this..."

Boru drew his.

They circled each other. Boru kicked a small table out of his way. Jorus pulled Aolwynd back and ran inside for help. The warriors came together head to head with a clash of their crossed swords. Boru reached out and clutched at Halduro's throat. Halduro pushed him away and slashed across the air with his blade, cutting Boru on the cheek. Boru wiped away the blood with the back of his hand and they circled again, eyes locked on each other.

They parried back and forth across the courtyard, countering each other's blows, their swords ringing. They stumbled trying to avoid falling into the coals of the fire pit. Boru backed away into the darkness where there was more room to fight, drawing Halduro after him.

Aolwynd stood on the steps clutching her hands to her throat, her feet shuffling, she fought off an overpowering impulse to fling herself between them.

With a great swinging motion Boru leapt out of the shadows, put his whole body into his next strike, turning like a top. His sword cut through Halduro's leather jacket and the shirt beneath to the flesh of his chest, letting the blood flow in a long gash. Halduro dropped to his knees, his head hung and his hand released the sword as if all his strength had been drained away.

"Watch him." Boru said walking past Aolwynd, pushing aside the gawking, terrified servants. He came back quickly with two of his officers. Jorus disappeared around the side of the house.

Aowlynd stood frozen to the steps as the defeated man gasped for air. He lifted his head and blankly stared at her with glazed eyes, cold as a fish.

Jorus brought the cart around and Halduro was lifted into it and driven back to camp.

"This is no life for you." Boru said to her without emotion as he mounted his horse and followed.

Faolan came running up the steps of the inn the next morning. His eyes were mischievous and he clasped her hands in his own. "We've patched him up, as best those butcher surgeons can and we'll send him off home to the capitol and the House of Good Women there as soon as he's well enough to travel. Back to Guardia! There he'll mend, worse luck! But I'm rid of him! Free! How can I thank you? My brother says if I know enough to defend a lady's honor then I'm too old for a nursemaid." He took her hand, kissed it, looking up into her eyes with that shy smile she knew even in this short time so well. Then he ran back down the steps like a child waving goodbye.

Although the noise from camp was no louder than before, she knew they were making ready to leave. She saw little of the soldiers by day and at night only the officers came and supped, then immediately went back to their duties. The siege towers were finished, so tall she could see them from her windows. When Boru came to her it was always near closing time and he left before dawn.

Meanwhile, the inn was busier than ever. Folk that had arrived without knowledge of the siege found refuge there sleeping in the hall until they could make plans to return the way they had come. Aolwynd was thankful the beds were filled once more. There was much to attend to.

Folpas was healing and beginning to make a fuss. He did not care for his house being splayed from back to front by "paying guests" and complained bitterly that he could not walk around in his robe or sneeze without running into some "foreigner".

Jorus went to work breaking through a side entrance. Through this doorway guests could travel a corridor that led only to their meals and back to their beds. Folpas was pacified by this but insisted on being carried downstairs during the daytime. A couch was fashioned in his study near the window. There he could watch the courtyard and the entrance hall. The hounds could not have been more protective than he.

Faolan visited him and took a great liking to Folpas whose quiet but observant demeanor matched his own. Together they studied ancient maps of the world and talked excitedly, discussing many of father's more obscure literary treasures. Aolwynd often heard their laughter and later her father's gentle snoring. Looking in, Faolan would be sitting quietly absorbed in his reading while her father slept soundly with a smile on his face.

Jorus and Aolwynd took to riding farther and farther afield to the farms and villages of the countryside in order to buy what they could. Meat and fish were especially dear. The markets in the city had closed, becoming pitiful and dangerous places filled with empty stalls and desperate faces.

One morning they drove north to a farm they had heard might still have things to sell. Aolwynd had never been that far before but knew the farmer's name. She heard he sold excellent chickens in the past and hoped to persuade him to sell her some if there were any left to be had.

The farmhouse was set well back against a tall cliff of unbroken rock. The farmer had used every bit of his land for tilling. His fields already looked gleaned of squash and cabbage. The cut stalks of corn stood like sentinels. His barns and stables were all in a line like little soldiers, some were even caves delved into a stone ridge with heavy doors secured over their openings.

Jorus pulled the cart up to the front of the house. Aolwynd climbed down and knocked.

"Farmer Middens?" she called into the gloom. The door

slowly opened. A woman stood wiping her hands on her apron. She nodded toward the side of the house and closed the door again.

They pulled the cart around to the first barn. Its doors were swung wide. Hay fell from high above into a huge pile on the floor. Tiny shards of gold floated about in the air.

"Oo's thar?" came a voice from the loft.

"It's your neighbors, Aolwynd Meliors and Jorus, of the Swan."

"Oh aye? Be a minute!"

There was a crash and a stout man clambered halfway down a ladder then jumped into the pile of hay. His smock billowed out like a mushroom cap exposing an enormous, pendulous stomach.

"So...what's yer business?" he said brushing off the chaff.

"Provisions for the inn. I'm looking for chickens and I've heard you have the best."

"I'm the only, you mean." he laughed. "There's naught left in the countryside this close to town."

"Please, I have coin."

"Ah'll bet you do. It's a good draw, that inn. You wait, this business'll pass an' you'll be more than alreet agin. Laying or for the pot?"

Aolwynd smiled. "What?"

"Chickens..."

"Oh...both if you have."

"We'll see, coom in't house." He jerked his head and they followed him to his home and into the darkness of the kitchen. A fire roared in the hearth. Something was baking. Mrs. Middens put a large jug of buttermilk on the table and three mugs, then backed her buttocks up against the warm oven wall and folded her arms. "Ow's yer dear father then? Give 'em our best an' hope 'E's on the mend."

"Aye, it's a bad business, pirates. I won't go int' city anymore, well, yah can't now I hear, anyhow." the farmer said. "Do you want any veg? Good. There's precious few ta buy anymore. Where they've all gone to, I don't know. Ah let the poor gleam mah fields...but where's the rest o'mah regulars? Oh, they're there alright but too scared or too broke ta' come all the way oot here, 'fraid they woon't get back in. Must be starvin' in their beds. When will the soldiers take it back? You must know." Farmer Middens gave Aolwynd a penetrating look.

"Why would I know?" she blustered, looking at Jorus.

"Ah...you be straight with me now lass, I'm straight with you. Your inn was headquarters even before the troops arrived. Like as not still is." He glanced over her head to his wife who was smiling broadly and nodding.

"I know nothing of their plans."

"Hmmm, well I hope they do sumthin' soon. Winter is comin' an' we'll lose half the folk to th' pest and the other half ta' empty bellies. Any road, I've a bargain ta' strike with you...five for the pot and three good layers, plus I'll fill yer basket with veg for a good price but you've got to do summit fer me."

Jorus and Aolwynd exchanged looks.

The Farmer jerked his head toward a dark corner of the room, near the fire. There was a figure there they'd not noticed before. Sitting on a stool was a young woman, her hair hanging in her eyes, her fingers playing with the fringe of her apron. She glared at them impudently, her lower lip protruding. "My daughter, Fila. Take 'er off me hands as a serving wench. I'll warrant you can use another one an' she's no good to us. Just sits and mopes all day since I dragged her back from the city. Saved 'er life I did! But do she care? 'No Pa! Let me stay!' she says!"

"She was a good tavern maid when she were there, she can be that again." the wife said stubbornly pushing out her own lip.

Aolwynd tried to protest but the farmer slammed his thick hands on the table top and pushed his bulk up from his seat.

"Reet!" he said and left the house.

His wife waved her dishrag at the girl as if shooing a fly. "Git oop stairs and collect yer things....Fila! Move!"

The girl rose sulkily and dawdled one step at a time till she was out of sight, then they heard the scurry of feet above them.

"What have we gotten ourselves into?" Jorus whispered as they filled the cart.

When they were ready to go the girl jumped nimbly into the back and stuck her tongue out at her father as they drove away. As soon as they had disappeared from sight of the house Fila climbed to the front and threw her arms about Aolwynd's neck, kissing her cheek.

"Thank you! Thank you! I'll be a good girl! Don't you worrit! I can serve, Ah'm strong."

The change in her was miraculous. She had washed her face and put her hair up in a little knot on top of her head with a ribbon. Her shift and skirts were clean and a tight black bodice showed off her figure nicely.

"I hate them!"

"Your parents?"

"Yes. I hate them. Treatin' me like a babby. Draggin' me home from me work just when it was getting' excitin'. I hate that farm. I'd a thrown meself off the cliff if I had to stay there a minute longer! Yer me saviors!"

"Good the Gods!" Jorus cursed under his breath.

"Do the soldiers come to the inn? Are they all as

handsome as they say? How big is yer inn? Is it busy? Where will I sleep?" She mithered them with questions all the way back.

Aolwynd had to laugh. "Was I as besotted with soldiers?" she whispered to Jorus.

"Murder." he retorted with emphasis, shaking his head while staring straight ahead at the road.

Gerda stared as Aolwynd pushed the girl in the front door toward her. "What's this then?" she asked garrulously.

"The new serving maid."

Gerda's mouth closed in a thin line and her eyes rolled up to heaven. "What next?" was all she said and grabbing the girl by the shoulder steered her roughly toward the kitchen.

8

A Morsel of Poison

Fila was all thumbs as she served that first night. Plates and tankards slipped and clinked in her hands, spilling ale and gravy over her apron. The comely young person was the talk of the tables however. Many an officer grabbed her apron strings to prolong their conversation or make her giggle and drop something so she'd have to bend over in front of them. She glowed with excitement. It was all Aolwynd could do to keep her from dropping her tray in awe as each new officer came through the doorway.

Gerda was "fair distracted" by her silliness and called her into the kitchen not once but twice to "re-arrange" her apron. Fila took the scolding that went along with jerking her about as if she hadn't heard a word. Her eyes were fixed on the doorway ready to fly back into the dining hall. "Don't be swaying your hips like a common little "hoor" in my house, Missy! As if anyone would look at a chit of a girl like you!" Gerda hissed as the girl pulled away. Fila just giggled and skipped from the room like a calf.

As the evening wore away, Faolan walked in and took his usual place by the fireside. This was his territory in Aolwynd's little kingdom, claimed by him on his first night at the inn. He liked the 'strategic vantage' it gave him of the whole room he told himself. He also knew Aolwynd saved his chair especially and would look to find him there. He basked in her special favors and attention. That night she brought him roasted chicken and mashed turnips with extra butter.

Fila was quick to take notice of the handsome youth. He was 'just her age' and she sidled up behind Aolwynd with a tankard of mulled wine. As she handed it to him, Faolan nearly dropped his plate. His eyes shifted away from Aolwynd's smiling face to Fila's. Fila immediately tossed her head and winked at him, leaning down and placing the tankard on the floor beside him. His eyes wandered lower to admire her breasts and figure. She ducked lower as well and met his gaze where it had strayed. His cheeks took fire, Fila grinned at him and he turned his eyes toward his plate mumbling "Thank you."

Aolwynd stood amazed at this performance...'Vanquished! I've lost my puppy. How do these things happen?', she mused.

Fila made sure she was constantly buzzing back and forth between the tables nearest the fire all that evening. She shot her glances at him but flirted openly with the other officers. Faolan seemed was in agony and could not take his eyes off her. Later she returned to take away his empty plate and refill his drink. She leaned slowly over him to do so, so close his breath was on her naked shoulders. The other soldiers watched with relish and jabbed each other in the ribs.

Aolwynd had had enough, however. She was just about to pull the girl out of the hall by her hair when Boru appeared in the archway.

Faolan waved him greeting.

The look on Fila's face as she turned around was not what Aolwynd had expected. All night every man who entered got a look of greedy perusal from Fila or a blank-faced judgement depending on who was young and handsome or old and uninteresting. But this was a look of startled recognition and furtive panic. Fila quickly hid behind Aolwynd and whispered to her that Gerda needed help in the kitchen. Faolan watched her scurry away with a mixture of regret and relief.

Boru smiled and kissed Aolwynd's hand as he came up to her. "I see they've started a game of dice..." he said to Faolan, ruffling his hair and sending him away. "Come and be with me for a little." he dragged Aolwynd off to a settle in the shadows of the hall. "I must borrow your man Jorus tonight, and your cart."

"Tonight?" she asked, expecting to be told more, but he just stared into the fire and held her close.

Finally he said, "He knows many ways into the city and can get me near the citadel without being seen."

Aolwynd knew Jorus had had a woman there years ago that he used to visit. She suspected it was a married woman.

Jorus found them late into the evening and together the trio walked out to the courtyard. The two men climbed into the cart, pulled their cloaks around them, covered their faces with their hoods and drove away. The stars twinkled in the cold night air, then all was covered by cloud.

Not until morning did she realize they were not alone on their journey. Covered by an old blanket in the back of the cart when they left were what they had taken to be empty baskets. There was nothing in the cart when they returned.

Fila was gone.

"There's the little whore for you!" Gerda pronounced. Aolwynd winced at the word. "Gone to the city where her pa tried to save her from! Good riddance. No good will come of it."

One good thing came of the venture however. Aolwynd had Boru in her bed before daybreak, sleeping soundly. Too tired to go all the way back to camp, but also too tired for anything else.

She buzzed about the house when morning came, letting him sleep in. With every chore she felt self-important, house-wifely, smug and comfortable. She hushed the servants and annoyed Gerda with his breakfast order. She brought him eggs, bacon, figs, bread and butter, honey and cold milk to drink. He ate leisurely, sitting by her fireplace wrapped in a blanket. 'Well, married couples don't make love every minute...this is a different kind of love, warm and caring, hospitable...' she thought as she watched him with selfish pleasure. Boru grinned at her like a spoiled child.

Gerda was in a sour mood. "Play act while you can..." she muttered as she took the tray from Aolwynd who would not let her through the door. Indeed Boru was gone again almost as soon as he finished the last fig.

Aolwynd pumped Jorus for information all afternoon but he would tell nothing about what they had done or what Boru's plans might be. The only thing he would say was he'd felt a movement in the cart around the time they had come near the East Gate, just before they'd turned off toward the sea. He hadn't paid much attention as he thought they'd gone over a rock. He knew now it was the girl jumping out of the back.

"She's had a cold night waiting for that gate to open."

"She's an idiot. Good riddance."

But it was not the last of her. Two days later Fila came mincing up the steps of the inn like a feral cat, tidying up her hair and smoothing her bodice and skirt. She flew at Aolwynd with tears gushing down her cheeks begging to come back. She seemed capable of startling, instantaneous, emotional transformations. She fell to her knees and Aolwynd had to peel her arms from about her legs.

Gerda came down the steps with her ever present wooden spoon. Fila saw her look and backed away scrambling awkwardly on all fours.

Without a word Gerda broke the spoon over the girl's back. "Now look what you've done!" Gerda showed more care for her weapon than any injury. "Why should we take you back you wicked basket?" Gerda yanked her up by the arm.

"Please Mum! I won't do it again! It was all on account of my man...I had to see him again! Surely you understand, Miss?" she said looking at Aolwynd. Aolwynd gave her a cold stare and the girl's demeanor changed again. Now she was sly and solicitous. "You understand a woman's heart...what we will do, what we need." She glanced at Gerda as if she were a withered piece of fruit.

"You'll scrub pots fer a month...*IF* we take you back, an' I'm not sayin' we will! An' doon't let me catch you waving yer tail at the men neither, you little cat!" Gerda said pulling her by the ear.

"Ow! Ow! Don't let 'er do that to me Miss..." and then other words were aimed at Aolwynd from the corner of her mouth so soft she almost did not hear them, "it ain't fair, not when I'm protecting you like, you an' yer captain."

Aolwynd stared hard at Fila. "Leave us." she told Gerda.

Gerda looked hard at her mistress, "*Doon't* tak 'er back... ahm warnin' you..."

"What did you mean by protecting us?" she asked Fila after Gerda had stomped off into the house.

Fila again changed her countenance. Now she was secretive, conspiratorial. She took Aolwynd's hand and led her shyly around the corner of the inn.

"I know who you are."

"Indeed."

"You an' that captain."

Aolwynd's heart jumped in her breast.

"You're the ones their lookin' for. The 'murtherers'". She said the word in a low lisping tone for added drama.

"Filthy pirate scum! We were defending ourselves!"Aolwynd corrected her, seeing no point in lying or pretending not to understand.

"Oh, aye!" Fila nodded fiercely.

"And what do you mean you're 'protecting us'?"

"Oh! I've said noothin' t'nobody! An' I could 'av... y'know...told them. There's a reward out you know, a good one."

"What do you want..." Aolwynd set her jaw.

"I want me job back is all...honest." Fila saw her chance and wheedled like a courtier looking up at the heavens as if to pray.

"How do I know you won't go flying back to the city first chance you get? Your man..."

"Oh, that's all over an' done with, Mum."

Aolwynd raised an eyebrow.

"'E's found anoother girl, 'E 'as." and with that she shrugged her shoulders, clearly thinking she'd made her case. She tossed a smile and sauntered up the stairs into the inn without waiting for another word.

A few seconds later a pot flew across the kitchen

landing on the floor with a crash.

The sight of the siege towers rolling slowly like beasts along the road toward the city was awe-inspiring and frightening at the same time. Teams of horses rigged together pulled the great instruments of war with men walking along beside them. The towers were wider at the base for stability but still the road was uneven and every curve took careful maneuvering. As they moved, deep ruts were left behind where the gigantic wheels dug into the earth. The teams were un-hitched and re-attached at the back as they made the descent onto the plain. It was a treacherous undertaking and hours passed by as a single tower made its way to its objective. If a tower tipped it would fall and smash, killing man and horse.

Next came the wagons with supplies of armor and weapons, then siege ladders carried by more men. Catapults with their own teams of horses followed. Finally a great battering ram hewn from a single tree was pulled along on heavy wheels.

Aolwynd watched from a crest by the side of the road. When she turned round she nearly tripped over Fila who was standing beside her.

"Ist' that excitin', in'it miss?"

Aolwynd blew a little air between her lips.

"Oh, aye...it must be old news to you...fightin', killin'..." she whispered as if she were sharing confidences like sisters.

Aolwynd grabbed her by the sleeve, her anger welling up in an instant. She surprised herself but it couldn't be stopped, panic mixed with love made her fierce. "Don't you talk like this again! Not to anyone! Not like you're sharing some joke...not like you're my friend!" She let go of the startled girl. "Now get back to the kitchen!"

Fila shuffled off, pouting and looking back over her shoulder.

Folpas' health continued to improve. He watched the parade of men and equipment with interest from his couch by the study window. Faolan was with him. Together they spoke heatedly and long of what they would do if they were in command. Her father quoted long-dead historians and directed Faolan where to find the scrolls of famous battles fought in Earden and in foreign lands. Folpas sang to him in his reedy voice, "The Lay of the Warrior's Field", a ballad of fallen heroes and their stand against The Darkling's army in ages past. Faolan sat, dreamy-eyed listening, his chin upon his hand, watching the soldiers pass by the gate.

Fila ran past the study doorway. Faolan pricked up his ears like a hound after a deer but when he saw Aolwynd his face took on a troubled look. He bowed to her father and left the house in a hurry.

"Come here, child." Folpas said, patting his couch.

"What is the matter father?"

"You read me as easily as one of my scrolls."

"Yes, like an old and cherished manuscript."

"Ah...but brittle and with much of the knowledge fading away." he laughed.

"But known by heart."

"Hmm... and it is of hearts I wish to speak."

"Father?"

"I have had a letter."

She looked on as he pulled a scroll of paper from an important-looking leather cylinder. The seal of the Supreme Guardian was pressed in red wax upon the lid which hung from it by a strap.

"It is from Halduro. He is healed of his wounds it seems. It is an apology for his actions."

"I misjudged him then."

"Wait. For there was no need of this letter, no need of official seals or even of communicating with me. I do not know the man."

"Then why send it at all?"

"Because of the seal. Any letter with this seal must have been read by the Guardian himself before it was sent."

"Lord Borchard?"

"Yes, child."

"But I still do not understand? What else does it say?"

"It says nothing of importance to me."

"Then throw it away!"

"Apart from the apology and a description of his stay in the House of Good Women, there is only praise for Faolan and his brother..." her father's words trailed off in such a hesitant fashion that Aolwynd thought she might scream.

"Tell me!"

"This worthless piece of parchment..." he dropped it to the floor. "has only one morsel of poison in it, and it is meant for you."

Aolwynd stared at the curled thing beneath his bed like it was a snake.

"He speaks of a noble marriage arranged for the eldest son on his return. He gossips on about the splendor of the match with a girl from one of Earden's oldest families and of Boru's honor and sworn duty to his country. I am sorry, my love. You have made an enemy in Halduro and through him, the Guardian as well. Faolan tells me his brother also received this letter. He was told to give you up, retake the city and leave for home as soon as possible."

Aolwynd laid her head down on the softness of her father's green silk coverlet and pounded it with her fists.

9

Faolan's Glove

The wheels of war and the trudge of soldier's boots moving away from the inn drummed into the night, invading her dreams. Images assaulted her of faceless warriors parading away, disappearing into clouds of dust as she stood, exposed to all in her shift with naked arms and bare feet. Somehow she knew they were all Boru.

In the morning she found a puffy-eyed woman in her mirror. Her nose was red and sore. Who was this person sitting at her dressing table, a scowl on her face? 'What a cunning way to stick in the knife and be rid of me.' she thought. A threat, for that is what it was, to herself, to her father... 'How great an enemy I must seem to them?' It gave her little comfort. 'The court must indeed be a nest of vipers if this is how they do business.' She pulled on a shawl and closed her window. Frost was everywhere and the sun was like a blood orange. She shivered. Finding a black wool gown edged with golden ribbing at the bottom of her clothes chest, she pulled it over her head. She brushed the crumbled lavender from it. It just fit her mood, dark and miserable. She left her hair hanging and watched as the kitchen cat jumped into the chest and settled on her things. Instead of shooing him out, she left the lid open with a shrug.

Gerda was chopping vegetables. She took one look at Aolwynd's costume as she entered the kitchen and laughed so hard she dropped the knife and had to hold her ribs. The old woman spluttered and choked till the tears ran down her face. Aolwynd exploded with rage and began throwing everything she could put her hands to. Crocks of butter, spoons and tankards projected across the room. Dishes broke on the tile floor. The hounds fled from the room, their tails covering their genitals.

Now it was Gerda's time to explode. "You'll get no sympathy from me! What did I tell you! Soldiers are all alike! Never any different! Tell them to leave and they leave! Tell them to march and they march! Tell them to die and they die! You've been a fool, you and your heart! You can march with it right out of my kitchen and tie it to his horse's tail as he rides away!"

There was silence for a moment as they huffed and puffed staring at each other, recovering their breath.

The cat came into the room, slinking around the wall and crouched in a corner pretending to clean herself. His eyes were like slivers of gold as he watched them. He loved a good fight.

Gerda leaned against the sink, her arms propped before her. After a short while she regained her composure. "Hoo!" she blew out a rueful breath. "Listen my girl.

What's the use of grieving. Your life's not over yet. A hard lesson is a lesson learned well."

The maids, Jorus and Bror, the kitchen boy, all stuck their heads around the corner at once.

Aolwynd looked up. "Keep out!" she yelled, pelting them with vegetable peelings.

She sat that night in Faolan's little chair, dreaming by the fire. Her hounds watched her nervously. There were fewer guests to serve now that the soldiers had all gone. A young man sat in the corner feeding his crow a bit of cheese. Two peddlers gobbled heaping portions of oxtail stew and called over and over again for more biscuits. Aolwynd watched them shoving the bread into their packs but she was too depressed to throw them out. A traveling minstrel strummed his lute absent-mindedly, drinking his ale.

Two more days for Aolwynd went by in this infuriatingly quiet fashion. She cleaned and brooded and everyone tripped over her. Even her dogs avoided her until bedtime when they insisted on crowding onto her bed. She put up with their sympathy until the lead weight of their bodies made the bed a trough and their snoring drove her to kick them furiously. Then they seemed to think it necessary to lay down with their haunches near the fire and their snouts pointed toward the door. There they stayed guarding their mistress from what ever might come.

On the third evening as she arranged meat pies upon the sideboard she turned to see Boru standing in the archway. A deer was draped over his shoulders. It was dark in the hall and the light streamed in around him. Behind him Faolan followed with the rest of Boru's scouts. They took up their usual places and Faolan almost ran to his spot by the fire.

"I'm that glad to see you all again." Aolwynd told them with a catch in her voice.

"I'll take this to the kitchen." Boru called out to no one in particular. Turning on his heel the legs of the deer swung wide as he stalked out.

Aolwynd waited for him to return as she served the men their dinner but he did not.

Faolan was over-kind, smiling sadly at her as he ate. He complimented the pie, talked of the preparations for the siege and how he hated the new camp, it was windy and un-protected.

She heard none of it. Going back to the kitchen she found Jorus sitting on a three-legged stool butchering the animal in the larder. Gerda was standing over him with a scowl on her wizened face. Aolwynd asked where Boru was.

"I s'pose I should be grateful fer the meat, but I'm not. He marched right in here and dropped this mess on my floor," Gerda clucked her tongue at the blood and gore on her tiles. "then he marched back out without so much as looking me in
the eye...the coward." The old woman stood proudly with her hands on her hips.

"Gerda!"

"Bastard!"

"Enough." Aolwynd sighed and went back to the hall.

Toward closing time the captain came back and collected his men. Faolan was sitting with Fila, holding her hand. She popped up when she saw Aolwynd. Reluctantly Faolan made his 'goodnights' to his new favorite. He squeezed Aolwynd's hand as he went past, glowering at his brother. Boru stood in the doorway for a few moments, looked at Aolwynd without expression, adjusted his cloak and left.

The great room fell silent. One of the hounds stole a bone from a table and a metal plate crashed to the floor. The sound rang like a bell in the empty room.

In a flash Fila's arms were about Aolwynd's waist. "Ooh! I'm that sorry, I am! I know all about it...Faolan told me. You poor bird! Men! We're too good for 'em! We give 'em our hearts an' they stomps on 'em."

Aolwynd choked, feeling sorry for herself and pushed Fila off her. "There's no use blubbering, go get a tray and feed what's left to the dogs. We'll finish cleaning up in the morning, I'm too tired."

"Yes, mum, hearts are fools, eh?" Fila's eyes told her she knew just how tired she was and why.

Aolwynd sat by her bed chamber fire for a long time watching the embers burn low. Finally she combed out her hair and climbed out of her apron and gown. She sat in her shift till the cold forced her into bed.

She woke to the sound of new wood being thrown on the fire and sparks crackling and popping. The casement window had been thrown wide and Boru crouched by the hearth warming his hands. She sprang out of bed and grabbed her robe. "You should not be here, my lord."

"So formal? You do not want me here?"

She walked to the door. "Your father's orders...I love my family and do not want his fury to fall upon them...and I do not want to be played with."

"I am playing?"

"Like a cat."

"You know better."

"I know nothing...anymore."

"Have I ever given you reason..."

"No sirrah..." she said cutting him off, "you have never given me any reason to hope, not by word or deed. You need not feel obliged to me for anything." She held the door open for him. "You should leave at once before anyone sees your horse standing in my courtyard."

"I thought..."

"You thought," she cried out. Closing the door she leaned her back against it. "you thought to stay one more night, bed me one more time. Why should I care? I'm only one more whore on one more campaign. How many girls have seen the rump of your horse riding out their gate? What am I after all, but food and drink and a bed warmer till I'm not needed anymore! Gerda is right, I was a fool." She turned away from him and pounded her fist against the wooden door. "Get out." she said huskily.

"You do not understand." he growled and turned her around by the shoulders.

She grabbed the lapels of his leather jerkin and shook him. All the anger and insult of the last few days came pouring out of her. His eyes went black as she vented her temper, pounding on his chest. She called him 'Coward' and 'Feint of heart' then pushed him away. "Go marry one of your gossiping ladies... this whore will have no more of you!" she choked out, laughing and crying at the same time.

"I cannot be seen with you and I cannot be without you! What am I to do? What am I to do?" His eyes welled with tears of sorrow or anger, she could not be sure which.

Embracing until dawn, not daring to speak for 'Goodbye' was all they had left to say to each other.

In the morning he was gone.

On her dressing table, a note unfolded read:

"You were right, I should not have come. What am I to do? Do not look to see me again."

It took Gerda's panicky voice at her door to get her out

of bed. Aolwynd unlocked it and she came rushing in. "She's gone off again, the sly little bitch! She's gone off with his brother on the back of his horse! He's showing her the troops or something…riding out of here as bold as a bullock! She climbed up there behind him like a proper lady going on a picnic! The nerve of that girl! I'll kill 'er! This is all your fault! You *know* that, don't you? You should never have let that wench back into my house! And that *man* has been here again!" The old woman said giving her words a special emphasis and Aolwynd an evil look. "I'm not so blind I can miss a pile of horse shit steaming on the flagstones. What else would have left that mess but that great black beast of his? By the Gods and Corruption!" Gerda pulled off her apron in a fury, balling it up and throwing it on a chair. "We've got to find them children before the soldiers do! We'd better send Jorus after them."

Aolwynd covered her ears with her hands and followed her out like a dumb animal. Gerda descended the stairs, a raving mad woman in a cloud of blasphemy.

Jorus was duly sent on their fastest horse and did not come back until nightfall. Trailing behind him on a lead was Faolan's mount.

Gerda screamed when she saw it. "We are all dead men!"

Jorus told of some fishermen who had seen the couple riding along the shore early in the morning but none had seen them since. The horse had been found wandering the beach. There was no sign of the couple.

Jorus was sent right out again to the camp with an urgent message for Boru concerning his brother. She waited up all night in vain for him. A courier and two guards rode into the courtyard as soon as it was daylight. The courier handed her a leather packet.

The note inside read:

"You and your entire house are under arrest.
The gardener is imprisoned here. You will be
tried for complicity in the kidnapping of my brother.
Do not attempt to contact me again."

It was signed:
Lord Boru, Captain of the Western Guardians,
in the name of Borchard, Supreme Guardian of Earden.

"Kidnapped?" Aolwynd cried.

The courier looked down coldly at her from his horse.
"We have this morning received a ransom note from the
pirates. They threw it down from the city walls stuffed into
one of Lord Faolan's gloves."

With that he turned his horse quickly and rode out of the
courtyard. Two guards locked the gate behind him and took
up their posts within on either side of it.

Pacing the floor of the dining hall all day kept Aolwynd
from going insane. 'How can I help? What is to be
done...what can I do locked up in this house?' Her thoughts
skittered inside her brain like mice across a floor.

Faolan captured, tortured? It was too horrible to think
on.

Gerda was in hysterics sitting at the kitchen table.
Folpas was barely able to stand but tried to calm her,
insisting she sit down. He hung onto the rung of her chair
trying to give comfort. Aolwynd entered and sat down
across from them. She had never noticed any tenderness
between them in all her days, yet here it was, a friendship
of nearly twenty years. Had there been more than that?
Perhaps, but her mind could not grasp it, not now. They
were all of them silent until Gerda suddenly rose to her feet
and began pacing.

"I'm going out to look for her."

"Gerda! What are you saying?" Folpas stuttered.

"She's out there somewhere dying, I just know it. I can feel it in my bones. They used her, that scum, they used my greedy little idiot to get his brother. That's what happened."

"Woman!" Folpas spoke with alarm. "The house is guarded! We are all under arrest. They will kill youThey will kill you if you even say that much aloud!"

"What do I care about that now? I could choke on a chicken bone tomorrow! God's truth! We look to be hanged anyway, sooner or later. We might as well get to the bottom of it. For her sake, find her, as well as our own." She looked at Aolwynd. And there was a light in her eyes. "There's only those two at the gate...I'll slip out somehow. I'm not leaving that girl out there alone."

"I'm coming with you." Aolwynd said quietly.

"Good the gods!" Folpas breathed.

10

Hearts are Fools

Dressed in grey, cloaked and hooded, the two women left by the new side door that led to the sleeping hall, their backs scraping against the wall. When they came to the garden gate Gerda spat on the hinges and slowly opened it. Aolwynd's mood was as black as the shadows they clung to, avoiding the moonlight. Fila's face and the face of the pirate's girl shifted back and forth in her mind. Confused but determined to go anyway, she did not know what they would find, if anything, or how they might help. But it was better than sitting in the kitchen and wringing her hands.

A small tool shed stood at the bottom of the garden. Once inside they had only to pry open the outer door, long disused, that led to the sea. Struggling, they pushed it hard on its broken hinges and it opened with a crunch. They

stopped, holding their breath but they were too far away from the courtyard gate for the guards to hear. On the other side was a path through the woods, sloping ever downwards to the rocky coast.

A small boat was tethered to a post on the beach. They hiked up their skirts and waded out, pulling the boat off shore. Aolwynd helped Gerda in and held the boat steady while she sat down. With a push she sent it out into deeper water and flopped into the prow.

"I'll row." she said, turning the boat with an oar.

"Make for the fisherman's huts past Rocky Point," Gerda called over the noise of the sea, "that's where Jorus said they found the horse."

Aolwynd's back was sore and her arms were on fire long before they reached the point. She rowed first to escape the shore, then to keep them on course and not be swept out by the tide she had to look over her shoulder and correct every few strokes. The current was strong. As they rounded a quay, small fires could be seen against the moonlit cliffs.

"They're catching them sprats, they breed in the sand this time of year," Gerda said. "tiny things...delicious, but devils to cook."

Torches flew like sprites up and down the beach.

They drifted into shore and pulled the boat up, then untucked their skirts.

An old man approached them. "We don't know yah lass, nor yer good moother, but there's only enough fer our families."

"Stay! We're not here for your catch." Aolwynd said trying to smile. "Do you know who found the horse on the beach?"

"Oh aye...Dano found it. Didn't yah lad?" he called to a boy. Dano had tousled hair, a shirt too big for him and was covered in sand up to his knees. "They want to know about the horse, lad."

"I'll take you! I'll show you!" he cried and ran off at a pace down the strand. The women tried their best to keep up with him holding onto their sodden skirts. After about a half mile a spit of rock jutted out almost to the water's edge cutting the beach in twain. The boy pointed but would go no further and ran off leaving them alone.

There on the other side, the city wall reached from a great height down to the sand. There was a small door hidden behind scrub trees and rock at its base.

"They must have hidden here and waited for her to bring the boy." Gerda whispered.

"How do you know all this?"

"Ah kin feel it...ah know it."

They cautiously lit their lamp looking for signs of a struggle but the tides had washed away almost everything. Yet there, near the bottom of the wall were the marks of someone crawling on their hands and knees. They moved the lamp closer.

"There's blood." Gerda said stopping her mouth with her hand.

They began to walk in a wider circle around the spot. Further on were the clear marks of someone's feet coming toward the bloody impression. Then they found a pair of footprints, one pair deeper in the sand than the other, as if dragging the other or helping them to walk.

The women gasped and looked at each other. They followed the trail. The sand grew drier as they climbed the dunes.

There was no mistaking where the path was leading them. Above the reach of high tide near a bank of reeds stood a lone fisherman's cottage. A boat was pulled up on shore and all was dark in the house. Aolwynd pounded on the door. A voice called from inside. "Allreet! Allreet! Ahm' comin'."

They heard muttered cursing, a candle was lit and then the door opened a crack. They lifted their lamp to expose their own faces.

A gruff young fisherman with black curly hair and a two day old beard looked them up and down. "What do thee want?"

"Have you seen a girl? She's in trouble, may be hurt. We are looking for her. We found a bloody path leading this way."

"Go away! There's naught here but me and me Mam."

"But the pirates..." Gerda blurted out.

"Aye, the pirates. Go get out of here before I call them dirty bastards ta murder yah."

"Jem!" came a woman's voice from within. "Let them come."

He squinted his disapproval but opened the door and yanked them both inside with a strong arm, looking out hurriedly before he closed it to be sure no one saw them.

It was a poor cottage. A table and two chairs made the kitchen and parlor. Near the hearth a mattress had been laid on the floor and an a woman was bending over it tending to someone.

They came closer and saw that it was Fila. She did not seem to see them, her head rocked back and forth in delirium. Her hair hung in damp little curls across her forehead. Her eyes were wild. "Got to get back to the inn! Got to tell them!" she clutched at the woman's hand. "Heart's are fools! You hear?" she spoke in a gurgling voice.

Jem spoke. "Mam found 'er spread eagle on the beach, face doon in't sand. 'Ow she managed ta' drag 'er all the way here I'll never know. They'd 'ad their way wi' her and then stuck the knife in fer good measure. Scum."

Mam nodded at the women and raised the blanket that covered the girl. Her stomach had been pierced by a blade, her clothes were torn and soaked with blood.

Gerda fell down on her knees beside Fila, her face a mask of grief. "You foolish... foolish child, what have you done?"

Fila's eyes grew wide and focussed on Gerda. "I...I didn't know....I didn't know...they promised me money." her hand searched and grabbed for Gerda's own.

"What were you thinking?"

"Forgive me." she whispered.

"You knew what you were doing..."

"Tell us where they took him!" Aolwynd cried, pushing close to the girl.

"Taken him?" her eyes wandered.

"Where did they take him, please Fila!"

She smiled at the mention of her name. Then her eyes widened. "My lady...my lady..." she gasped for air, "the garrison!" She put something inAolwynd's hand. Her breathing became raspy, gurgles sounded deep in her throat. "Forgive...forgive..."

"She's fading." Mam whispered.

Gerda pushed Aolwynd aside and picked Fila up in her arms, weeping. She held her as a mother might, rocking her like a baby till she passed.

"Servants of the gods, come for her now." Jem prayed, touching his forehead with two fingers, then his lips and chest.

"Help us get her back to the boat. I'll not leave her here, not my little bird." Gerda pleaded with the young fisherman.

They were a sorry sight traveling the length of the beach. The moon went in and out covered by clouds as the three of them walked along the strand. Jem carried Fila wrapped in a blanket as if she were a sleeping child. Aolwynd marveled at the strength of him for he did not seem to mind the burden. He appeared to be whispering or talking in Fila's ear as he carried her, like a father, reassuring her that everything would be alright in the next world. Gerda walked silently next to him, her back hunched over with despair.

The crowd on the beach had disappeared, all that was left of their harvest were tiny pock marks in the sand.

Fila was laid in the prow of the boat out of the wind. Aolwynd thought of her father as he lay curled up on the ropes in the pirate's skip only a few weeks before.

"Ahm coomin' with you." Jem said looking out at the water. "You'll never make it back yersels'." The sea was turning and the tide was strong, white caps ruffled on the waves like wings.

They didn't argue with him.

Gerda settled herself. Jem and Aolwynd pushed off. She jumped in with soaking skirts and he jumped in after her. With one last lunge of his strong arms he sent the craft out into the waves. Together they rowed, though she was no match for his strength, she tried to keep up. His years of skill and his well-muscled back were gods gifts that night. They surely would have 'wrecked on the rocky shore without him' she thought. The wind was chill and her knuckles were white with cold and exertion. Her palms felt as if they were frozen to the oar.

Jem knew every inch of the shoreline and sought out and found the path to the inn long before either woman could recognize it. He let the tide carry them in the last few yards and it was with a great sense of relief they heard the sand and pebbles scrape the bottom of the boat.

Gerda led the way up with her lantern covered, only the

bottom illuminating the path to the top of the cliff. Jem followed next, carrying the body of the girl and Aolwynd climbed the path last. She kept an eye out for signs of movement from above but it was long past the shank of the night. They followed the garden wall to the back of the stable and slipped inside. Aolwynd opened the doors as quietly as possible and peeped around the edge toward the gate. The guards were still sitting at their posts, their heads nodding with sleep.

Once inside, all was cold and dark. They made up one of the pallets and laid Fila down, covering her with a clean, dry blanket from the stores. Gerda made sure her eyes were closed and her arms rested on top. Then they crept quietly into the house.

The shutters were closed in the kitchen and Bror had stoked a welcome fire. It seemed stifling after the freezing winds of the sea. Aolwynd's hounds tapped their tails sleepily but did not move from their spots on the hearth stone. The kitchen cat stretched and yawned, jumped to the counter and sat staring at Jem.

"You must stay the night, you can sleep in Jorus' room, we will think how to get you back in the morning." Aolwynd said.

"Get me back?"

"Yes, we are prisoners here. House arrest." Gerda smirked.

Jem's jaw dropped as they told him their story. While he listened Gerda fried eggs and bacon. She kicked the kitchen boy awake and made him toast bread. Aolwynd found three tankards and filled them with wine and spices then stuck a hot poker from the fire into each of them. The wine hissed pleasantly and gave off the aroma of cloves and cinnamon.

Jem smiled and sniffed the air. "This is a grand place..." he sighed.

"It were, afore it were a prison." Gerda grumbled.

They sat in silence, eating their breakfast and drinking the wine. Slowly their hands and minds began to thaw out. Gerda sat glaring into the fire, stacking and unstacking the little pile of foreign coins Aolwynd had set on the table. The gold glinted in the firelight. The faces and inscriptions were unknown to them but they knew where they had come from. This was Fila's reward and her death, clutched in her hand as tight as a vise and never relinquished even after she was attacked.

When they finally admitted to exhaustion they showed Jem to his room.

"Thank you. How can I ever repay you?" Aolwynd sighed.

Taking a candle from her hand, he lit it from hers and said "No need." Looking down into her eyes he closed the door ever so quietly.

11

Sage and Mistletoe

In the morning Jem was anxious to leave.

"We will give you a horse." Aolwynd told him. "But please. You must do me one last favor. Ride to the guardian's camp before the city walls. Find the officer's tents. Ask to speak with Lord Boru. None other. You must speak to him alone. His banner has a green spiral emblazoned upon it and his shield is round with many studs like a bull's eye. It will be hanging outside if he is there. You must tell him how Mam found the girl and all that had been done to her and you must give him the coins she had." She put a pouch in his hand.

Jem and Aolwynd slipped back to the stable and although she would have given him any one of the three fine horses they owned he chose a sturdy beast, shorter than the others and shaggier, more like a pony, made for carrying and pulling.

"I make you a present of him, Jem, with our thanks."

Jem smiled handsomely, his grin at once broad and shy. "He'll be a big help to us, we'll take good care of 'im."

Together they saddled, bridled and stealthily led the pony to a little path around the back of the compound. Jem rode off and into the trees.

Aolwynd hurried back to the courtyard. A few minutes later she smiled as the guards ignored Jem riding past them like any common traveler heading for the city.

It was afternoon when the sound of galloping horses and men's voices made Aolwynd run for the gate. She jumped back just in time as Jorus came riding in, his hands tied in front of him. He was accompanied on either side by a pair of riders. They helped him off the horse untying his hands. One of them approached Aolwynd and taking hold of her under the arm walked her forcefully up the steps and into the inn. He closed the heavy door in her face.

She ran to Folpas' study window, Her father drew aside the curtain just in time to see Boru ride in with two officers. She was shocked to see his face. He was troubled as if he had not slept. Anger, worry and a kind of buried panic all played their part in the way he glanced about, the way he jumped down from his horse and the way he carefully avoided looking at the house. He kept his eyes on the ground as Jorus led him to the sleeping hall.

They did not stay long.

Folpas held Aolwynd's hand as she waited for Boru's return. The sun fell upon the green silk coverlet and its shiny surface hurt her eyes. When Boru came back from the hall he turned his horse so that in mounting he would not have to face the windows. He leaned over and gave some instructions to the guards at the gate then rode out with his men.

Aolwynd sat on the couch, all the breath knocked out of her. Folpas stroked her hand. "We do not always have answers, my love," he whispered, "and we cannot always see what lies ahead, but until we are dead it is not over, believe me."

Toward sunset a cart pulled up on the road and to everyone's surprise the guards let it in the gate.

It was Farmer Middens and his wife. Aolwynd ran down the steps and made to embrace them. They shrank away, sullen as stone, deadly quiet and pale in the face as if all the life had been drained out of them. The farmer croaked out a few words as if he had been struck with feeble-mindedness. His wife showed nothing of what must be welling within her except for her trembling lower lip and the kerchief in her hands which was damp and knotted from twisting.

Aolwynd led them around the house to the sleeping hall. They stopped a few feet from its doors. Almost, it seemed, they did not want to go in, as if that last step would bring about the death of their daughter and they would have been the cause.

The double doors were swung wide and a shaft of silver light made Fila look like some ancient queen carved in stone. Gerda was sitting beside her, almost in shadow and Aolwynd guessed that the old woman had been there all day. Gerda's lips were blue with cold but she made no sign of discomfort. Fila's hair had been combed and dressed and lay about her shoulders in long golden ringlets. Set about her head were sprigs of ghostly sage and mistletoe. A clean woolen blanket of cream color covered her corpse. Her white arms lay above the coverlet and in her hands more greens and sage were put. Gerda had placed spices around

the body beneath the blanket.

Aolwynd nodded to her in thanks while holding back her own tears.

In a little pile on the blanket at Fila's feet were the gold coins.

Farmer Middens reached out instinctively for his wife as she fell to her knees next to her daughter's body. She let out a wail that sent the kitchen maids running from the house. They stood in a clump by the door moaning, like mourners and holding each other.

Jorus brought their cart around. Aolwynd helped the wife to her feet as Farmer Middens and Jorus took either end of the pallet bed and carried it outside. The two guards came forward from their posts and together the four men lifted her, pallet and all, into the back of the cart without disturbing her rest. Mrs. Middens was helped onto her seat.

"Thank you for bringin' our girl back to us. We'll put that gold in the hole when we bury her." Without another word the farmer climbed up beside his wife, turned the cart and rode out of the yard.

Gerda and Aolwynd held hands as they went back to the inn. Aolwynd nodded her thanks to the guards.

Morning brought another leather packet from the captain. The messenger did not wait to take back an answer.

"Aolwynd," it read,

"it seems I cannot trust you to understand what it means to be under house arrest.

Thanks to you and your stubbornness, no... your foolish courage, (did I set that free in you?) I now know where he is hidden, though I do not know how I will get him out. The fisherman seems to think highly of you, (Where did you ever find that oaf?), as does the farmer. I will intercede for your servants and family but Halduro is coming back with orders from my father and he will surely see you hanged.

I must find a way to help my brother and you, I am desperate, I am torn in half."

There was no signature.

Jem came the next day riding his pony past the gate. Aolwynd pretended to pay no attention to the traveler but taking her time strolled out of sight of the guards. Sprinting behind the stables she met Jem as he reined in his steed.

"Whoa Sprat! I feel a proper gentleman riding up to you like this..." he joked. With a warm smile he dismounted, throwing his leg over the pony's back.

"Come in and we will make you something to eat while you tell us why you are here."

"Aye. I've summit to tell ye'."

They settled at the kitchen table. Gerda presented him with a plate of fried sausages and apples cooked just through with nutmeg and ale.

"So?" Aolwynd sat, watching him eat with a look of patience growing thin upon her face.

"I were out tending to my nets yesterday when two of them bastards come walking right up the beach at me, bold as puppies. They asked me did I know anythin' about the girl that were killed t'other night. The scum. Like we doon't know what happened to her. Ah' asked them how they knew there was a girl there at all."

"Oh Jem, that was dangerous."

"I don' care. I'd of stuck 'em both right then and there but I knew you'd want to know all about it. An' if I'd'a stuck 'em I'd'a had ta disappear like, eh? Maybe not see you for a while." Jem reached past his plate toward Aolwynd's hand but pulled back shyly and reached for his tankard instead.

"Any road, they said she'd stolen some gold and they wanted it back. The dirty bastards. Said there was a reward for information."

"We know what that gets you." Gerda said.

"Thank you, Jem. I'm glad you've come. The stars were all in a pattern when we met you." Aolwynd said smiling. Jem blushed and hid his face behind his drink.

Gerda's eyes shone sharp as an owl's and she sat down across from Aolwynd. "Aye. But 'E's done enough." she whispered.

"No." Aolwynd breathed. "Jem, I have need of you again, if you will. But I must warn you, if you help me, I will draw you in deeper, I am still accused, there will be danger, but maybe tales the city will tell for years to come."

"Maybe sad tales." Gerda moaned softly as she got up and poured herself a brandy.

"I cannot guarantee the outcome but if we succeed we will give the army the help it needs to rescue The Guardian's son and begin to re-take our city. But this is your choice and I do not lay anything upon you."

"Oh yes you do." Gerda mumbled as she poked the fire.

Jem put down his drink and laid his hand on Aolwynd's arm. He squeezed it gently as if judging its strength. "I will help you lass, any way I can, ah' think you know tha' already." His eyes looked deep into hers.

Aolwynd broke his gaze slowly and looked away with embarrassment. Taking a deep breath she said "Good. All that is required of you for now, is to take a message to The Banker that I will write. You must go into the city and say you have information about the gold that was theirs. Say you must speak to The Banker."

"Oo's 'E when 'E's at home?"

"He is their leader, I think...anyway, he keeps their money. Once you deliver the message, remember, only to him, you will be able to get out of the city safely, he will insist on it. Now finish your meal and I will write my note." She left them drinking, silhouetted against the orange flames of the hearth.

"Pushy, ain't she?" Aolwynd heard him say with a chuckle.

Folpas was sleeping in the study when she entered, sat down at his large desk and took quill to paper.

The first note read:

"To The Banker,
So, your men would have back their paltry coins from the fist of a murdered girl? I do not have them, they lie at the bottom of her grave. Let your dogs dig them up, if you dare, may the gods curse them for their sacrilege. I have a bargain to make which will be much more to your liking, I must go to my father's warehouse, there are papers and records of his trade that we must have if we are ever to start again and there is gold there too, though you would never find it. Also I would like to take any stores of spices which were left before they spoil. I will split everything with you and pay you for the spices I take. It would make you a rich man. You need not tell your ship mates for I will not say anything. I cannot believe a man like you does not have some plan for the future? With my help perhaps you can achieve it?
If you agree, send word with Jem and I will meet you on a night of your choosing at the warehouse.
Come alone.
"Aolwynd of The Swan"

Then she quickly scratched another note and returned to the kitchen.

12

A Loop of the Rope

"This is suicide, my love." Gerda said as she finished reading the note to the pirate. "You do not believe for one moment that this filthy brute will keep his word?"

"Of course I do not. All I hope is that he will believe that I am foolish enough to bargain with him and that he is greedy enough to double cross his companions. Once he is inside the warehouse the game will change. I will have my revenge for what they have done, and I will start with him."

"Yes, and he will kill you or worse, take you off and you will wish you were dead, like Catalina." Gerda muttered, shooting down another brandy.

"That is where Jem comes in."

"Ah!" Jem said, his eyes twinkling in the firelight. A hint of a smile crossed his lips and he pushed his fingers through his dark hair.

"Gerda, I will need you also."

"Thank the god that protects all fools, I thought for a minute you were going to tell me to stay home and bake pies. I can be stubborn and foolish too, you know. But surely this is not your whole plan? This is little better than vengeance and a suicide note. Where is our escape? How do you send word to the soldiers?"

"Patience."

"That dog will have men waiting around every corner even if he does plan to play by your rules."

Aolwynd pushed the empty brandy bottle with her finger. "As for what we do next...it will not matter how many rats are hiding outside in the shadows. Leave it at that for now. Trust me. There is one more piece I must put into play."

"What's this? A game of Kings Men, my love?" Folpas walked in leaning heavily on a cane. "You speak of my favorite game and I am not a part of it?"

"Yes, we were talking of your beloved game." Aolwynd said looking hard at her fellow conspirators.

"I do not think we have met, sir?" Folpas extended his hand as Jem stood up.

"Jem has made us a present of some fish. He is the man who got us safely home the other night."

"I thank you, sir. Do you know the game?"

"Nay. But I have always wanted to learn."

"I will be your teacher! Come! Let us set the board!"

Jem looked back at the women with sheep's eyes as Folpas took him by the arm and teetered jubilantly across the hall. An hour later Jem returned, his eyes bright but dazed.

"It's a king's game and no mistake. Give me your message, I must be out 'o here before he wakes up."

"One more thing," Aolwynd said, holding Jem by the sleeve as he walked. Jem turned his head and looked down at her taking her hand as if they were strolling in a garden. Aolwynd lowered her head, then looked straight in his eye. "Jem, please, ride once more to camp and give this note to my Lord Boru. Tell him I have news of his brother and must speak to him. He will not like it and will think I am pleading to see him again. Tell him, no, I am in earnest, that you know of what I speak but will say no more."

"*Your* Lord Boru, eh? Not meet with you? Then he's a fool. I would not turn down an opportunity to tryst with you, not ever." Jem looked solemnly at her, turning her hand over and back again, admiring the smooth skin and slender fingers.

"I can never thank you enough." she said pulling her hand slowly out of his.

Jem grabbed an apple from the wooden bowl in the hallway and made his way to the stables.

She dressed carefully as the sun went down hoping and yet not expecting Boru to come. She put on a wine-colored gown over an under dress of yellow silk that she saved for special occasions and dressed her hair simply with a ribbon of red. She told herself she did not want him to think she was pining away or sat tearing out her hair covered in ashes. Then she went downstairs and waited.

Two guardsmen rode into the courtyard leading a spare horse that evening as the sun set.

"Come with us." was all they said as they bound her hands in front of her and lifted her onto the horse. They rode on either side reaching out every so often to steady her as she wobbled in the saddle. She clung with both hands to the pommel, her heart pounding, trying to keep her back straight and ride like a lady. Trying also not to think of

Halduro, of hangings, nooses and executioners.

As they entered the camp, children ran along beside her throwing clumps of dirt and calling her names. The women she had so admired jeered and cursed, her dear soldiers, who were scattered amongst the others only turned their backs or lowered their heads. Only one met her gaze, Boru's Second, the man, Tanner who stood guard outside the tent. She kept her eyes straight ahead, could not look at him and tried not to cry.

The banner with the green spiral curled lazily in the cold breeze of evening. Tanner helped her down and whispered to her to wait inside.

Alone in the tent, Aolwynd walked about the space and could not help bu be curious. It seemed unusually small, then she realized it was divided into two halves by a flap. She peeped in the back. Boru's sleeping cot stood at one side and did not look to have been used, a studded wooden chest piled high with clothes thrown there in a hurry stood against the other side.

In the anteroom, maps of the city were strewn across a table, and there were two chairs and a stand for wine and cups. Empty bottles lay beneath everything like dead men. To the side was a wooden rack as tall as she was. It held his long fur cloak with the silver buckles. She ran to it and grasped the rich fur, drinking in its deep scent and holding it close to her. The smell of his own scent was heavy on it from long use. It was his favorite thing, she knew, beyond his sword and shield. It drew her even closer to tears.

Boru was standing in the doorway, silhouetted, dark against the light of the campfires. His mood was dark also.

"What do you want?" he growled.

She jumped back letting go of the cloak.

"I must talk to you."

"Get out."

"Then why did you send for me if not to hear me out?"

"Haven't you done enough? I've thanked you, go back to your house, you are still under arrest." Turning away he whispered, "Why do I fall for your tricks?"

"This is no trick."

"Guards!" he called. Two came running in.

Aolwynd stuck out her chin and took a deep breath. "I will say what I have to say, you know I will...if I have to scream it from the back of a horse. Why not hear my plan?"

Something in the tone of her voice and the way she stood toe to toe with him made him relax and smile in spite of his mood.

"All right, have your say." He waved the guards out. Pouring himself a cup of wine he sat down at the table. Offering her a cup he smirked and she held up her bound hands in reply.

"I am going to set fire to my father's warehouse."

He put the cup down and stared at her.

"That is not all. My father's warehouse is like a strong box, I doubt they were able to pillage it. It is built in such a way that there is a row of boat bays accessible to the harbor. His goods are off-loaded easily within the building itself.

Jem tells me the pirate ships are all anchored together quite close to the piers now and that the sea dogs have become comfortable, planning to stay the winter, living off the citizens and their own plunder...I plan to set fire to their ships as well."

Boru's eyes glinted in the flame of the candle. "You are such a fool...where does it come from..."

"Wait! Once the fires are lit you will see the flames in the sky from anywhere in the city. The scum will panic and some will doubtless leave their posts at the garrison, perhaps at the gates as well. It should be enough of a

157

distraction."

"Go on..." he said, his voice just above a breath.

"Jorus will get you back in the city, you and your men back to garrison by streets he knows well. This will give you a chance to rescue your brother."

"What do you know of the garrison?"

"It overlooks the harbor with only one entrance facing the sea. At its back the walls are blind to the streets as its only duty is to defend the harbor. Chances are, the entrance will be abandoned when they run to save their ships."

"I cannot let you do this thing. It is too dangerous." he said but his eyes told her without words that for the first time in many days he had found some hope.

"I will do it anyway, whether you will or no," she smiled. "and Jorus will be waiting at the garbage gate to take you in. Use us or we will die trying to save your brother and our city."

She stood in front of him leaning over the table with her bound hands upon it. "Use us...I would rather die there..." she pointed to the harbor on his map, "than by Halduro's rope." She talked in detail then, everything she could think of that might happen but she did not mention The Banker's part in it.

"I will send word with Jorus when I know which night it will be."

"I do not even know if they've kept him alive." Boru murmured.

"He is...for Jem heard the pirates complain to each other that the captive eats better than they do."

Boru laid his forehead down upon his arm and let out his breath. When he raised his head again his face was relaxed and his spirit seemed cheered. He stared at her and shook his head.

Coming around the side of the desk he cut her bonds,

took his cloak from the stand and threw it over her shoulders.

Come, we must get you home, my love." He walked her out holding her arm, it was hard for her not to stagger. Her knees were like water.

Tanner waited near the tent, holding Boru's horse. She knew he must have heard them but his eyes revealed nothing.

Aolwynd blinked up at the night sky. All the children had been driven inside to their beds and for that she was grateful. The campfires had burned low. High up on the walls of the city, torches were moving slowly back and forth where the pirates stood their watch.

"I will take her back." Boru told Tanner who nodded back at him, keeping his eyes down.

Both arms were tight about her waist and his cape covered them both as they rode slowly through the quiet camp.

The road to the inn was silver in the moonlight and the trees were like black lace stripped of their leaves against the winter sky.

"I've...I've missed you so..."was all she could say, her voice catching in her throat.

He turned aside into the woods. "My flower." he said. He knelt upon the ground, wrapped his arms about her knees and held onto her tightly. To Aolwynd, suddenly, he was a little boy.

Sighing, he looked up at the stars, "My brother..."

13

A Note Sealed With Wax

Two days went by without a word from Jem.

Aolwynd paced about the house fussing and rearranging things that were good enough as they were. She swept the courtyard till there wasn't a leaf to be seen. The wind blew more into the yard and she swept them over again. She brought the guards hot drinks and pretended not to stare down the road. They watched her with amusement. It was all over camp that she was Boru's woman and that she was going to die in spite of it or because of it more likely. Halduro did Borchard's bidding, they knew, '...or more like t'other way around.' some whispered. They reasoned the buxom innkeeper was going crazy with fear at her impending trial with the hanging sure to follow.

Gerda tended to Folpas who was anxious and spent much of his time in her kitchen where there was more to distract his mind. Aolwynd's moods were easy to read and when she was silent he knew something was about to happen, something he could not prevent no matter what he said. She had seen Boru, so whatever was coming would likely be far more dangerous than the last time. He peeled Gerda's vegetables out of frustration at his daughter's willfulness till the old woman complained he had pared them all down to 'nubbins'. He dutifully drank cup after cup of her medicinal tea in recompense but it did little to calm his nerves or hers. To take his mind off things he told Bror tales of the dragon that lived beneath the Guardian's city. The boy's eyes grew wide as a pigeon's and he begged for more.

On the third night Jem unexpectedly sauntered into the kitchen.

Aolwynd nearly dropped a pan of gravy in her surprise and relief.

"Ahm back." he said sitting down comfortably in the chair nearest the fire and throwing one leg over the arm. Reaching for a piece of uncooked beef from Gerda's cutting board he popped it into his mouth as if he'd lived there all his life.

"A pleasure to see you again, my boy." Folpas said with a glint in his eye.

Jem clapped a giant hand to his heart. "Your honor."

"Jem, may I see you a moment?" Aolwynd asked, drawing him out into the shadows of the hall. "Don't say anything of our plans, I don't want to worry him."

"Like 'E doon't know already, eh?" Jem toyed with the shoulder strap of Aolwynd's apron. "Doon't you see him lookin' yer way?" Jem sighed. "'Ow about tellin' me, 'Glad ta see yah, yer looking well, Jem. They didn't cut yer throat like I thought they might, eh?' Ah well...soldier's girl...tha's what I hear, any road." Jem let go the ribbon. "Nah then, there'll be a whole sight more to worry about if we don't none of us come home..."

"I know." Aolwynd mumbled gazing back at the kitchen doorway.

"Aye, well, it went like you said. I got int' the city tellin' 'em I knew about the coins, then I told 'em I had to see The Banker. They didn't 'alf get fired up about tha' but I got 'em to take me to 'im, after a while. They all seemed scared of 'im and tha's good. He was in a guard house joost by the garrison so I got ta see how many and where they were stationed-like. They're all spread 'oot. They're not as many as an army but they're mean an' they doon't care if they slit yer throat fer a penny. They've got the city folk cowed...not but if we get them started I think they might rise oop an' fight. They're near starvin'."

"Jem... The Banker?"

"Oh, aye. Well, I gave 'im yer message an' 'is eyes lit up. 'E closed the door so no one else could hear us talk. 'E must 'av read tha' note five times. Then 'E said 'Yes' with a smile on 'is ugly pan of a face. 'E'll meet you in five days...there's no moon tha' night. 'E'll meet you alone, like you said."

Aolwynd sent Jorus to the camp with this information, then they sat down at a table in the dining hall to go over their plan. After a time Jorus came back with a message and Boru's pledge to be ready. He placed an object wrapped in cloth into her hand, she did not open it for she knew what it was. Boru had sent a gift of his dagger.

Jem was told to come again on the fourth night for they were going to get there ahead of time.

Jorus and Gerda put their heads together making a list of supplies. Tinder boxes and flints were gathered from all over the house. Torches were made of dry pine needles and strips of cloth dribbled with pitch, wrapped tightly into a bundle covered with oil cloth. They would take food enough for two days only, if they did not succeed there would be no need for more. Gerda filled jugs with water and added her lantern to the pile that was already growing outside the back door.

Folpas took to his bed again, coughing, exhausted by suspicion and tired of their denials.

Aolwynd dug clothes for their journey out of her father's old wardrobe. She dragged leather breeches, shirts, jackets, belts and coats to her room. She tried on outfit after outfit like a child playing dress up and spent her breath trying to convince Gerda to wear the same.

"If I'm gonna' die I'll die as the gods fashioned me, I'll not go to mah grave in a pair o' troos."

The maids were scandalized by Aolwynd's choice of clothing and thought her mad with fever. She settled on a cambric shirt cinched in by a belt and leather breeches. She reckoned she could move better in the out-sized shirt and it hid her breasts. She buckled the dagger to her belt and turned around.

"I would rather die as a man." she told them as they left the room too afraid to giggle or talk her out of it. Aolwynd took her manly things off and piled them neatly on the bed for later.

Jem arrived in the afternoon of the fourth day. The women went down to meet him on the shore with the first load of supplies. He had scrubbed the barnacles off the hull of his own boat and pitched all the seams anew. It was beautiful to behold, they told him. He grinned with pride. He had set in an extra pair of oars and a length of rope. Up in the prow, stowed away safe from the wind were three inflated sheep's stomachs painted with pitch. "No use gettin' drooned." he said.

They ate in leisure in the kitchen with Folpas at the head of the table. He was surprised to see his guest but Jem told him he'd come to play another game of Kings Men. Folpas accepted this answer knowing full well Jem had some part to play in the danger that was to come.

"Don't make sheep's eyes at me, you asked to be taught to play." Aolwynd whispered to him.

Gerda presented them with a meat pie the size of a hog's head and a jug of wine sauce to go with it.

"How will we ever row after this?" Aolwynd grumbled.

Jem's eyes were wide with hunger as he cut himself a massive slice, then he served everyone else and kept the platter to his side of the table. "Boatmen need their strength." he said between mouthfuls.

Folpas laughed for the first time in many days and they all made a merry feast. It was so long since there had been any joy in the house that Aolwynd counted it as the first of many blessings and a good omen. They whittled away at their meal, laughing and telling tales until there was half a pie left on the platter.

"Well, I'll wrap this up." Gerda said signaling by a nod of her head that Jem had better have his game if they were to get Folpas settled for the night before they left. Jem looked like a lamb led to slaughter but Aolwynd only laughed as he followed Folpas across the hall.

Jorus came in from the cold. He'd been to camp again, studying their maps and going over the last details. Boru had been busy, he said. He had gathered together his band of scouts, Aolwynd's own dear soldiers and told them of the plan. When they learned of her part in it they were silent and guilt-ridden for doubting their Swan, but it fed their resolve. Boru swore them to secrecy, showed them the corrected map and their path to the garrison. They were concerned for Aolwynd's safety and worried Jorus very much over the details of the parts that were not known to them and the many things that could go wrong. When they

166

were done, every man knew his position, every turn in the route they were to take and where every corsair and sea dog was placed in the city.

Jorus sat down heavily at the table. Gerda placed a plate of food in front of him but he only pushed it away. "Give me a brandy, I have to check on my mead." he said gruffly. Looking at Aolwynd he whispered. "Come with me."

They walked to the ale house Jorus had built with his own hands and he lit a candle at the door. Leaning over his tubs of mead, he lifted their lids and peered in, then he bade her sit down. "I should be going with you tonight." he said.

"You cannot be in two places at once, my sweet man. You must guide Boru and his men."

"In fact, I should be going instead of you..."

Aolwynd glowered at him.

"if anything should go wrong..." Jorus said quietly, taking her hand, "set fire to the building and kill yourself and Gerda...do not be taken alive by the enemy. They will try to use you as leverage...then they will use you in ways too horrible for me to think on. Even if you are dead they will lie and say you are hostage. Promise me you will not give them a chance to lie. If all goes ill you will know and do this thing. Do it for those who love you and that way I can tell your father and Lord Boru they are lying...for they both must have some peace, after a time."

She threw her arms about his sun-tanned neck and promised. "Of course...of course. What am I to do with all of you? Your trust...your courage..."

"And yours, little Swan." Jorus stood up. "It's time we rescued Jem and finished loading the boat."

Aolwynd climbed the stairs to her chamber feeling very unsure and small. Fear crept up the stairs behind her, un-looked for and unwelcome. The size of the endeavor

168

suddenly overwhelmed her. She took off her gowns and dressed in a kind of dream. Her hands shook with cold as she cinched in the belt and fastened the dagger's sheath to it. She took out the blade and saw how it gleamed in the candlelight. Sitting down in front of the mirror she looked at herself. Slowly she unwound the long black plait of hair and pulling it up tight above her head, she cut it off. Then she cut her hair all around till it was shorn close as a sheep.

Gerda came in with a pair of shears. "I thought you'd do something stupid like that, by the gods and mirrors!" she breathed. "Let me make you look less like a thistle top!" The final effect was very short but somehow flattering. They smiled at her reflection. "You are quite a boy now! But remember, even boys are not safe from those filthy pirates, nor safe from soldiers neither for that matter."

Her dark humor gave Aolwynd courage and they walked down the steps together, arms about each other's waists. They laughed so hard that Jorus and Jem came running from the kitchen.

The men stood like two baby birds with their jaws open, staring at Aolwynd's clothes and hair. Jem recovered first and grinned from ear to ear rubbing the stubble on his chin. Jorus was not pleased but as there was nothing he could do about it he threw her a package of torches and headed for the door.

That night Gerda put Folpas to bed in the study. He was too tired to go upstairs from the heavy meal and the game with Jem. He had fallen asleep easily and was snoring gently as Aolwynd tip-toed into the study and sat down at his desk.

This is what she wrote:

"Beloved father,
In the morning you will find us gone. Jorus will look

after you. We are going to set fire to your warehouse in the hopes it gives Boru the opportunity he needs to enter the city and rescue his brother. Forgive me. Then, my love, we can win. If we fail we will have still succeeded in trying to save our city and we will have redeemed our good name.

          Know that I love you. Aolwynd

Within this note she placed another one, folded and sealed with wax, for Boru.

14

Olive, Almond and Sesame

It took longer than expected to make all things right but finally they were ready to leave. Gerda jumped up and down at the back of the boat to help lift it off the sand as Jem and Aolwynd pushed off. Jorus stood on the shore, a solitary figure getting smaller and farther away with every stroke of the oars. As they passed the headlands he was still standing there and Aolwynd prayed to the Sea Maidens and spat in the water asking that he might be there to greet them upon their return.

It was indeed a dark night and the moon was gone. Even so, the tides played with them, pulling the boat out and making Jem correct their course. Every fifth stroke he had Aolwynd hold as his powerful arms dug his oar deep into the waves pointing the prow back in the direction he wanted, following the shoreline. In this way, like a water bug skimming across the surface, they managed to zig and zag along the coast. Jem kept track of his many landmarks, rocks and sunken wrecks, calling out their names as they went.

"How do you know all this?" Aolwynd shouted over the wind.

"Oh I think I could find me way in me sleep. I've walked it, swum it an' sailed it since I were a wee sprog. Thar' ain't a rock or a sunken post I doon't know of."

"Glad we are of that!" Gerda shouted above the wind.

Clouds passed overhead, the waves buffeted them and they labored on. After a time the pale walls of Saels came into view but no movement was seen on its ramparts and they continued on.

"There's Mam!" Jem pointed. As they glided past her cottage a small figure in black stood looking out at the sea. The woman raised one arm over her head in greeting, then went back into the house.

"What did you tell her?" Aolwynd asked.

"Everthing, innit? Always do. Noo secrets from Mam." he said.

"Too late now." said Gerda.

"She woon't talk." he said proudly.

Around the shank of the night the shoreline curved northwards. They began to see houses and docks built closer together. They passed under a causeway of tall pilings and suddenly the water became calm as a pond. They were in the canals and waterways of Docktown, a whole neighborhood of fisherfolk, sailors and ship builders that had no need for streets.

"Let's stop a moment and rest." Jem said. They tied the boat in the shadows of a taller craft and listened. Some houses still had lamps burning. Noises and laughter echoed across the water and dogs barked but there was no one on the canals.

"It can't be too bad fer folks here, they haven't started eating their dogs yet." Gerda whispered.

"Doon't be daft woman, there's fishermen here." Jem scoffed. They drank water from a shared jug and waited. One by one the lighted windows went dark and candles were carried upstairs by tired inhabitants. A window opened and a chamberpot splashed its contents nearby.

They covered themselves with cloaks and pushed out into the maze of channels leading to the harbor. It took them another hour to navigate through the dense neighborhood, avoiding posts and boats tied to the docks.

At last they saw the open expanse of the harbor with its cluster of pirate ships at anchor. They were indeed sitting close to shore and some of them were even moored together with ropes to the wharf.

"We canna risk rowing too close, they will surely have set a watch an' they might see us or hear us. Which warehouse is it?" Jem asked, taking off his coat and pulling his shirt over his head. He handed them to Aolwynd with a smile and a wink.

She pointed to the largest structure on the wharf with four dark recesses at the waterline. "There is a pier attached to the side, we can hide the boat beneath that."

Tying a rope to the prow, Jem threw the other end in the water and slipped silently over the side. Treading water rather than swimming he pulled the boat ever so slowly within the shadows of the wharf until they came at last to the warehouse. Aolwynd shivered with cold just looking at his exposed skin in the water. Gerda did not take her eyes from the ships lest they were discovered but all was quiet.

Beneath the warehouse pier, Jem climbed out and began to unload. There was a narrow stone ledge that gave them

just enough room to creep along without being seen. Rats scurried out of their way as they inched along the building to the entrance.

Aolwynd got her father's keys and unlocked the heavy metal entrance door. The sound of the lock turning seemed incredibly loud and she winced with fear it might be heard.

Gerda pushed her inside and closed the door. "The first time I'm glad of drunken debauch..." she whispered. "They're all in the 'sleep past caring.'" She lit her lamp. The cavernous warehouse exploded with light. It took their eyes a few moments to adjust. Reflections twinkled on the water surrounding the four boats each bobbing softly in its bay.

"I hope Jem is alright, the water is so cold..." Aolwynd said, remembering with surprise the glimpse of sleek muscles working steadily beneath green water.

"Jem's a fish, he'll be alright." the old woman sniffed.

"Douse the lamp, I hear him." Aolwynd said. Gerda covered it with her shawl and opened the door.

Jem came in with an armful of provisions and went back out. "Well, we're here." he said when he came back for the last time, dumping the supplies on the floor.

"You're fair blue with the cold." Aolwynd said throwing a blanket over his naked shoulders and rubbing his back and arms hard to get the circulation going. "Did anyone see us, do you think?"

"Nought out there, too late, too cold." he said through chattering teeth. "Th...thank you." he turned away from her clutching the blanket and smiling shyly like a maiden.

Gerda coughed and rolled her eyes.

Aolwynd stuck her tongue out in reply.

They sat huddled in the small circle of the lamp. Jem pulled on his shirt with difficulty but his hands were too cold to fasten his jacket. Aolwynd reached out to button it for him and found her hands suddenly clumsy and her cheeks growing warm. Jem watched her hands as they struggled and looked up at her with a curious expression.

"Let's get to your father's office, it will be safer and warmer there away from the water." Gerda stood up and adjusted the lamp.

Yellow light bounced off the walls and the smell of spices mingled with the brine of the harbor. The scent of cinnamon, cloves, pepper and cardamon intoxicated their senses as they moved back through the aisles. They could taste as well as smell the air. Barrel after barrel, pot after pot, row upon row of tall shelves filled with culinary treasures marched back through the enormity of the warehouse. Little curling paper labels lay strewn about on the wide plank floors amid sesame seeds, rat droppings and rose petals. Vermin squeaked and scuttled in the dark beneath the shelves.

"It's like a bloody fortress in here." Jem whispered pointing out the barred windows at the back punctuating the stone wall with small squares of pale night sky.

Next they passed large amphora filled with oils: olive, almond and sesame. Strings of fragrant star anise hung in great loops like necklaces from hooks as did dried red and green peppers.

Lastly reams of silk in many colors lay stacked upon great viewing tables. Their threads of gold in patterns of flowers and birds glinted as the trio passed by. Aolwynd remembered her childhood spent sitting beneath these tables or running between the shelves laughing at the ladies in expensive gowns who came to buy and fought over these beautiful fabrics.

They walked under a narrow balcony on the south wall and climbed the stairs leading to Folpas' office. It was perched like an eagle's nest high above the stores. From here the whole expanse of the warehouse could be seen.

Aolwynd opened the door and breathed in the aroma of her past. Her father's desk stood piled high with ledgers just as he'd left them. The air in the room was close and stagnant. Brass plates with decaying spices sat waiting for his approval and small vials of aromatic oils.

"Phew!" Aolwynd waved her hand in front of her face. She motioned to Gerda to cover her lamp again and went to the only window, opening its heavy shutters just enough to let in the fresh air and to tell them when daylight broke. "Let us try and rest after we've eaten, we'll need our strength again tomorrow."

"If yah doon't mind I'll finish tha' pie now." Jem didn't wait for an answer but sat down and was as good as his word.

They settled down on blankets rolled out on the floor. Jem curled up like a ball with his knees tucked up trying to warm himself. Aolwynd threw her blanket over him and cuddled up with Gerda beneath hers. After a time Jem's legs stretched out and he snored, exhausted. The women lost more and more space in the tiny office for Jem seemed to expand and unfurl like a vine as he relaxed, a leg here and an arm there.

15

Rose Petals, Sandalwood and Flames

Morning came first with the chirping of birds, then a grey light. Specks of dust floated in the air like shafts of moving silver illuminating the vast interior of the warehouse. A cool breeze came in through the office window and Aolwynd crawled over the floor to close the shutters.

Jem and Gerda were snoring, competing tunefully with their mouths wide open. She had to laugh. Standing up Aolwynd rubbed her arms, hugged herself and walked onto the interior balcony. The a stronger sun light fought through the small barred casements, slicing yellow stripes along the floor and climbing up the shelves.

This was Folpas' empire stretched out before her. The

complete representation of his years in commerce to vast and exotic lands. Sacred friendships made with chieftains and kings, cagey bargains with brigands and pirates, contracts honored with all the peoples of the world, these shelves held the history of his life. And she was there to burn it all. She leaned over the rickety balustrade, staring solemnly at her father's precious, rotting, empire of stuffs.

A hand covered her own.

"It's a good plan." Jem said quietly. "Don' over think yerself. Coom back ta bed." he whispered, chuckling softly at his own joke.

When they'd all slept enough that the hard floor wore patterns into their backs, Gerda got out the remains of the food and they ate breakfast in silence. Figs, hard cheese, bread and butter did not seem nearly enough for Jem but he didn't complain. They descended the staircase, listening to his stomach rumble. "I make it about noonish. We'd better get them boats loaded." he said.

It took some arguing till they decided how best to structure what would in essence be floating bonfires. Everyone had their own opinion on how to make the perfect blaze. The warehouse itself was easy, anyone could run down the aisles with a torch and set it alight, but the boats...they had to be set out at the last. How to make them blaze up quickly, burn long enough to reach the ships and not burn out, that was the question. What if they just bobbed along in a wind and never reached the ships? Would spices blow upward like sparks? Was that a good thing or did it mean they would fly away into the air and not land where they were asked? Would the reams of silk be better on top? Which oil was best? That was the only easy answer, all oil burned. Finally they came up with an elegant combination of their shared ideas.

Then they set to work.

In the hulls of the four boats they laid pieces of wood from the shelves creating a platform that a draft could get under. Then a layer of silk to prevent the shards of her father's precious sandalwood from falling through to the bottom. This was good tinder and made the next layer. Then they piled more reams of fabric soaked in oil at either end leaving a spot in the middle to start the fire. This they filled with more sandalwood shards and all the spices they could find that were dry as twigs. Finally they covered everything with empty wooden boxes and casks to hide the scheme.

When they were finished the boats looked as if they were left, waiting to be unloaded. Gerda filled several smaller jugs with oil, putting them nearby in readiness for the night and placed the torches in holders on the wall. She would have to light them quickly from her lantern and she didn't want any fumbling.

It was getting late, the sky turning orange and the light in the warehouse was growing dim. They sat on the floor and planned the arrival of their guest.

"He surely expected you to come through the East Gate with your cart, when he has no word from the guards that you have passed through, what will he think?" Gerda asked.

"I don't care...I'll tell some lie...he will come."

"What if he's got men with him?" Jem asked.

"Oh! I can't think anymore! I've brought you both here and I only planned to die if I had to, I guess I didn't plan it out very well, all I've thought about is revenge...it's not about the city...it's about my father!"

"Oh, aye...There goes his warehouse, as might 'av lasted till the pirates were all gone...sweet revenge tha'." Jem said softly.

"I'm no soldier!" Aolwynd cried rocking back and

forth."Stupid! Stupid!" she repeated angrily, getting up and moving further away, throwing scraps of wood into the water.

"It's alright." Gerda said. "We'll think it through. I never thought we'd even get this far!" She stuck out her tongue at Aolwynd.

Jem threw his arm over Aolwynd's shoulder. She buried her face in his warm neck. With a look of surprise he hugged her. "Nah then...we'll see it done." he whispered.

'I've heard that before...' she thought.

As soon as the sun set they raised the boat doors even with the surface of the waves. Aolwynd lit a lamp in her father's office and set a strong box on his desk with a wine bottle with two glasses. She began to get jumpy, her pulse racing. Time was running out.

Jem found a hiding spot for himself near the stairs and Gerda took her place by the warehouse door.

Aolwynd slipped out, not meeting Gerda's eyes, locked the door and went around the corner into the shadows to await her guest.

It was damp and cold near the water and it made her shiver. She kept fingering the hilt of Boru's dagger. Her courage was at its lowest ebb. Then she remembered something her father had read to her from one of his favorite scrolls. It told the story of an ancient battle and of the men who fought in it. It read: 'Fear walks with Courage, for they are brothers and both are blind. If Fear goes first and Courage follows all will be well but if Courage goes first and Fear comes up behind both will be lost.' This steeled her heart and she began to look around listening to the sounds of voices carried across the water from Dock Town. Men were laughing and women were singing. Life went on its way, with or without pirates.

Along the pier she saw a figure approaching. She

recognized The Banker by his badly-dyed hair, blacker than pitch, it made her smile. He had decked himself out with a red sash and new boots for her benefit. He seemed to be gesturing to someone to keep behind him, waving a large hat with a plume. Then she saw them, two men, following at a distance, keeping a slow pace, craning their necks and looking about them suspiciously.

Slipping around the corner of the warehouse she leaned against the side near the entrance as if she'd been waiting for him there all along.

As he approached his expression showed anger and confusion, scanning the wharf he was looking for a woman. Suddenly, he broke into a broad smile.

"Well, well, well. What is all this then?" Coming right up to her with his foul breath and livid scar, he bowed and swept his hat through the air meaning to impress. Toying with the buckle of her belt he gave her a tug towards him. Her knees shook beneath her but she screwed up her courage and smiled.

"We have business I think. And you were supposed to come alone, like me."

"No 'Good Evening, Sweeting.' for me?" He purred. "Oh don't mind the boys, them's me body guards. 'Ow ever did you get past the gates in tha' outfit? Clever girl. Aren't yah glad ta' see me? Ah' knew yah liked me first ever ah' saw you."

"Business." Aolwynd gulped nervously.

"Ah, yes...business." he breathed but he was not put off his course. "I like yer hair, very becoming, no place fer bugs." He tousled it then stroked her neck with his hand, leaning in to her. She felt the wall against her back. There was no where to go.

"Let us go inside and talk. I have wine and we can strike a bargain."

"Ah'd like noothin' better. After you, my lady...or should I say 'my lad'?" he laughed and slapped her backside.

Out of the corner of her eye she saw the two men lounging on posts near the water's edge, not even bothering to hide any more. She unlocked the door and cast a smile for their benefit. To her relief they stayed where they were. When The Banker was in, she closed the door.

"Leave it unlocked." he said.

Nonchalantly she hung the keys on a hook knowing Gerda would quickly make her way out of the shadows and lock it.

The Banker looked around warily with his hand on the hilt of his sword. He did not like being closed in. It was obvious only greed or lust or both, more likely, were driving him on. He jumped as they passed the silks for they fluttered with every movement of the air. The rats however, did not seem to mind him.

As she came to the office stairs he took her arm and held on tight. He moved up with her stepping as she stepped, like a lover, whispering in her ear ways he knew of pleasing her as they went.

"Now let us spend a pleasant evening together, my Aolwynd, my bird." Nothing about him disgusted her so much as this mention of her name from his lips. They entered the office and he closed the door, scanning the room. "We will need two more glasses for you are entertaining meself and me men th' night."

"I told you to come alone..." she backed away slowly, fumbling with the leather flap on her dagger's sheath and hoping he could not see it in the dim light of the oil lamp.

"Ah...no one will be coming alone tonight, my love. We're all going to be great friends before this night is over."

She grasped the dagger and pulled it out. He sprang at her and quickly twisted her wrist till she dropped the blade crying out in pain.

"You're a right vixen, aren't you?" He smiled as he walked her backward like a dancer.

"Our bargain..." she squeaked, her voice breaking in fear as the back of her legs hit the desk. She tried to distract him.

"Have some wine, luv. You'll need it, unless you've poisoned it, av' you? Here, we'll see, shall we? Too bad for you, if ye' 'av." He picked up the bottle and shoved the lip of it into her mouth, hitting her teeth against the glass in the process. The red liquid poured down her throat and neck and onto her shirt. "Oh...I've spoiled yer clothes and ye' dressed so carefully fer me, too..." He pulled her leather jacket down over her arms locking them at her sides then ripped the collar of her shirt down over her shoulders. Grazing her neck with his lips and teeth he murmured. "Good girl..." Her skin crawled and she shuddered as he reached into her shirt. "How you guessed my mind in your note...so sweet of you, me darlin'. Yes, I have plans for a future, a house in the desert lands, across the seas, already bought, just waiting for me there, with servants, when I'm through with all this." He took his hand out of her shirt and waved about the room. "Am I such a villain? Look at me...Why not join me there? You're a woman of spirit, I can tell."

Aolwynd turned her head away.

From the warehouse below came the sound of banging and shouting. His two companions had tried the door and found it locked against them.

"What have you bin up to, eh?" he whispered holding her at arm's length. "Who locked that door?" He slapped her hard across the face and she slid to the end of the desk.

"Just my maid."

"You broke yer bargain then as well. Tell er ta let them

in then, an' quick!"

Aolwynd made her way clumsily around the desk as The Banker gripped her by the front of her jacket. He opened the door a crack. She called out "Gerda! Let the two men in..." She had just enough time to see Jem hurrying behind the long row of shelves rushing toward the entrance.

"Come 'ere, we're not finished yet." The Banker said, pushing her back into the room where she nearly toppled over, unable to use her arms. He took up the wine bottle and kicked the door closed.

"Don't you want to settle our bargain first?" she asked, trying to put the desk between herself and the pirate. She glanced at the strongbox. He flipped open the top. It was full of coins. His eyes strayed to the gold but only for a moment then they came back to her naked shoulders.

Aolwynd gulped.

He took another drink. "Aye. I'll take that an' more but first I'll take you."

There was little room for her to move and still trussed up, she panicked, scattering papers and spices everywhere. He saw the fear in her eyes and was on her like a dog on a chicken.

The sounds of a struggle coming from the floor below grew louder with shouts, curses and clatter. Gerda had let the men in and Jem was fighting with the pair of brigands.

Aolwynd heard the door slam and hoped that Gerda had managed to lock it.

The Banker grabbed her hand, twisted her round and walked her to the desk with his arm about her neck. He finished the wine and threw the bottle to the floor. With his free arm he swiped the ledgers off the desk and reached around for her belt cursing all the while. He pulled the belt tight to unbuckle it as she screamed and struggled. He bent her body over the desk and yanked at her trousers.

"Guess they must be hav'in a dance w' yer maid...by rights Ah'm first anyways, lovey..." The pirate drove his knee hard between her legs, hitting bone and knocking the wind out of her lungs. She saw stars and yelped with pain.

"Jem!" she cried with the last of her breath.

"You bitch! Who else is here? You'll die fer this after I've...!"

She tried to move with every ounce of her strength but his body held her in place as he fumbled with his own trousers.

"You keep still or I'll cut ye' deep right now an' it'll be the only hard thing you'll ever feel agin!"

Suddenly she heard feet running up the stairs and Jem burst into the room with a pirate's cutlass in his hand.

The Banker pulled her upright by the seat of her pants, swung her away and pulled out his sword. "She's dead if you move, fisherman." The pirate spat and looked around, judging his distance from the door. He backed toward it with Aolwynd between them forcing Jem to circle out of his way.

"Tyke! Zook! Whar the gods are ye?" he yelled out the door but no one answered. He backed slowly onto the balcony pulling his victim after him.

Gerda was hiding behind the door. She threw her lamp onto the floor below and it burst into flames. The Banker jerked around, startled. Aolwynd kicked him in the shin as Gerda came round from the shadows and grabbed hold of his sword arm. Jem leapt out of the office and The Banker let go of Aolwynd. She fell, tumbling ass over tit down the length of the stairs. She lay at the bottom in a heap, on the verge of unconsciousness, her head reeling. From the floor above she heard rather than saw a violent struggle. Three shadowy giants danced across the ceiling as yellow light flickered below and grew bright. Their black figures twined

and swayed, wrestling as two, then three, then one great tumbling shape.

Gerda screamed. The rungs of the balcony broke away and The Banker fell to his death on the floor. Flames began to climb the bottom shelves of the warehouse, leaping from plank to plank all around, illuminating the sprawled body of the pirate.

Aolwynd sat up holding her head in her hands, then she saw Jem carrying Gerda down the steps toward her. Her arms hung limp and Aolwynd took her hand as he laid her down on a work table covered in reams of silk.

"Gerda! What has happened?"

Gerda's eyes smiled.

Jem spoke softly. "She hit 'im wi' the door when you fell, it gave me a chance ta run 'im through but 'E turned on 'er and with 'is last breath 'E sliced 'er good. The bastard! She grabbed 'im then, bless 'er lion's heart, an' I thought they'd both topple over tha' railing but I hung onto 'er so she wouldn't fall."

"Gerda! No!" Aolwynd wailed.

"Get out, Sweeting..." Gerda breathed. "You an' Jem have to finish this business now, get out while you can."

"No! I won't leave you!"

"Listen child. Leave me. Finish them." Gerda closed her eyes.

The air was already thick with smoke, it was hard to breath or see anything. Gerda lay like a queen, a corpse surrounded by golden fabrics with billows of scent from roses and sandalwood engulfing her like incense.

Jem grabbed Aolwynd's arm and together they ran for the boats. The air was a little clearer near the entrance but not for long. They raised the boat doors one after another pulling on the ropes. The winches screeched with rust. More air from the harbor came rushing in. Flames from the back of the warehouse flashed up and over the ceiling curling and roaring toward them. Panic caught Aolwynd by the throat and made it even harder for her to breath. From the back of the building they could hear the large amphoras exploding one after another. Flames bright red and yellow, fed by plumes of oil reached for the roof, finally piercing it and chasing each other up into the night sky. Support timbers began to crackle and fall. Soon the main beams would give way.

Aolwynd crawled over the boats and lit them with a torch while Jem sawed away at the tether ropes. It took what seemed like an eternity before they were all bobbing freely. The stuff in the hulls flamed up as soon as it was lit.

Voices were screaming outside and calling to each other from all over Dock Town. People streamed out of their houses and along the wharf carrying buckets.

"Leave off tha' boat an' get out of here!" Jem called to Aolwynd. Moving from one bay to the next he shoved each vessel out into the harbor.

People were shouting as Aolwynd rushed headlong into the crowd. They were all screaming at once. Yelling at the top of her voice over the roar of the fire, she told them to let it all burn. She pointed to Jem who was swimming behind a boat in an attempt to guide it toward the pirate ships. It took only a moment for them to understand what was happening. Immediately men made for the water. Diving in, they surrounded the flaming vessels. From a distance it looked like the boats were propelling themselves, white foam kicked up from the swimmers feet splashing behind them. The crowds began cheering. Then they went to work moving boats out of the path of the fire and dousing the nearest houses with water.

Aolwynd heard a tremendous crack as the great beams of the warehouse began to fall. It was now an enormous fiery monster that reached into the sky. No doubt it could be seen from the east. The smoke of sandalwood lifted her prayers for Boru and the soldiers. The taste of burning spices and hot peppers burned her lungs.

She explained between fits of coughing what was soon to happen at the citadel and the citizens ran back to their houses to get weapons. She heard the shouting of the pirates from across the water as the boats afire drifted into their ships. The flames exploded, higher than a man and took on a new burst of strength from the hidden reserves of oil-soaked wood in their hulls. Fire quickly climbed up the sides of the ships. Jem and the men swam back to shore through a flurry of arrows. The sea-dogs were trapped with no time to un-moor or weigh anchor. Screams came from the seaward side as they jumped into the water. On the surrounding docks men and women were waiting for them with clubs.

Jem climbed up onto the wharf. He leaned over with his hands resting on his knees and cocked his head to one side smiling, gulping air and looking for Aolwynd. His hair was wet and his shirt clung to his skin. His chest heaved with exertion. His eyes glowed with pride.

The crowd ran this way and that in the chaos bumping into each other and cursing. Aolwynd heard none of it but ran up to Jem and threw her arms around him. They clung together in the middle of a crush of frenzied people, motionless, their eyes shut as the pirate ships disappeared into the bay.

Suddenly, behind them, with a low rumble, her father's empire collapsed. Timbers crashed and sparks flew. A last plume of acrid smoke ejaculated into the sky as the sun rose and crept across the whole area covering everyone with ash and filling their lungs with it. Jem kept Aolwynd from falling to her knees, holding her tight in his arms. Her grief for her father and Gerda came back and overwhelmed her. Jem dragged her away from the wharf and into the crowd running from the inferno.

As the ships were burning they heard yelling from the garrison high above the harbor. Voices carried and they saw tiny figures running down the street toward the water. Perhaps two dozen brigands had panicked, abandoning their posts. Waving their weapons, the dogs came sprinting down the embankment. Not all had left their positions but enough came running to bleed their guard and give Boru the chance he needed.

Jem lost no time rallying the harbor folk. He had turned into a captain himself, giving orders and pointing toward the enemy. Aolwynd marveled at the strength still left in him after all they'd been through.

As for her, she crept out of the way, ashamed and exhausted, too shaken to do any more than fall on her belly, catch her breath and cry. Coming through it all she had forgotten the true reason for her actions and that the burning of her father's warehouse and Gerda's death was not the end of the fight but only the beginning. To her shame, she just wanted to crawl away, sleep and forget.

16

The Underworld

Jem found her leaning her back against a post by the water's edge hypnotized by the last wisps of dark sweet smoke hovering over the harbor. She was thinking on the end of Folpas' world. Bits of what had once been pirate ships floated in the yellow waves like the shards of sandalwood.

"Coom on!" he yelled, wild-eyed with excitement. "So this is battle, eh? Ah could get used ta this. Coom on, we're headed up the hill!"

"I...I can't. I can't do this any more. Our boat, you'll come back for me."

"Oor boat is burned ta bits...its all of a piece with that muck in the harbor." His eyes looked toward the crowd, their small leaving him behind. "Get oop!" he tugged at her arm. "Ye can sleep when yer dead!"

"I am dead...I'm..."

"Coom on luv, ahm not leavin' y'here!" he said and giving her a vicious yank he kissed her quickly on the cheek and half-carried her till she found she was running beside him.

The mob met the pirates who had abandoned their posts at garrison head on, knives and clubs swinging. Like some enormous many-headed beast whose thoughts were shared instinctively the mob parted as the brigands ran amongst them. Before they knew what had happened they were surrounded by a circle of harbor folk eager for vengeance. The scum had no choice but to close ranks, fighting back to back in a little knot but it was a desperate, futile defense and soon ended.

Several of the Docktown folk were killed but none of the pirates survived. All were bludgeoned to death or stuck through like pigs. Their bodies were heaved into the harbor as they had done with their victims, accompanied by the curses of the mob.

Without a word the crowd turned and picking up the weapons of the dead began to move up the hill.

As Aolwynd and Jem joined the mob, shouting and the clash of swords could be heard from the garrison. Everyone began to run again and she found she was running along with them. A fierce burst of energy returned and carried her along. Jem grinned as he saw this and let go of her hand. He ran ahead into the crowd and was gone.

To Aolwynd's great relief she saw the glint of soldier's armor amongst the fighting outside the open gates of the stone fortress. The mob washed up in a wave and joined the guardians, flooding into the garrison's courtyard where fierce fighting had already begun. Aolwynd was carried in with them. The flag stones were littered with the dead, slippery with their blood and it was hard to go forward without climbing over limbs and bodies. 'What is my business here?' she thought, looking around, suddenly confused, sapped of strength once more. Picking up a cutlass she made it her job to help who ever seemed ill-matched in the fray. Many of the women were strong but hesitant fighters. One on one the pirates often out-maneuvered them, laughing and swearing. Aolwynd came up behind where she could and swung the blade begging Gerda to intercede with the Twin Gods of War and make it a swift kill.

Jem was at the head of a small band of men leading them up onto the ramparts. Their clubs and swords were raised as they chopped through the remainder of the pirate's watch, pushing the bodies over the precipice onto the streets below.

There was fighting in the covered porch leading to the guard rooms and lights moving in the archways leading down to prison cells below ground. She prayed Boru was there and that he would reach his brother in time. Staring at the torch light rushing back and forth behind dark pillars, she lost track of her business and was suddenly struck on the head. Falling backwards over a body she collapsed against a stone wall. Everything went dark. 'Finally I can rest…' she thought crazily and somehow in her mind, she became Gerda. Everything around her was in flames.

The reek of corpses and blood mingled with dust filled her nostrils as she slowly came back to her senses. Her clothes were wet and she only knew she was alive because her body shook with the cold night air. She could not tell which was worse, the shivering or the throbbing in her skull. Nauseous, she gagged on her own vomit and turned her head, dribbling it from the corner of her mouth only just managing not to choke on it. She tried to remember where she was. Still crushed against the stone wall she tried to wriggle out from under but had no strength left to move the many bodies that lay on top of her. Nor could she stand the fetid outpouring of the bowels and bladders of the recumbent dead. Overwhelmed, she faded back into unconsciousness.

How long she lay there she did not know but voices began to filter down from above as if she were in deep water. The sound of cart wheels came rolling over the paving stones, at first she thought she was in her own courtyard at the inn. Then the solid thud of bodies being swung into the cart told her what was happening. The fighting was over and the victors were removing the dead.

'Who won? Do I care? Am I dead?' she thought. 'Perhaps I am...if so, this is indeed The Underworld and it is not some place beneath Earden but present amongst the very living. To hear them, smell death all around me and not be able to speak. Yes, perhaps it is amongst us all the time. A question worthy of one of father's philosophers.' Her mind driveled on from one insubstantial thought to the next. There was nothing to be done. She would be thrown into the sea with the other soldiers and sea dogs or perhaps separated out and dumped in a mass grave or burned on a pyre. She hoped for a soldier's funeral and not a pirate's.

Then she remembered Gerda. Aolwynd let out a groan of despair.

"Oy! Thar's summin' alive in there!" a voice cried out.

"Over 'ere!" another voice called and the pile began to shift.

She let out cry of pain as the weight of the bodies moved onto her legs. Then she saw through eyes caked with blood...a little light.

"'E's in 'ere! Get 'em oot!"

Strong arms pulled the remains of a soldier off her and two other corpses were rolled away. The pale light of dawn and a chill wind off the sea hit her face, she gasped, breathing clean air once again.

"Get 'im in tha' t'other cart."

Two men carried her, picking her up by feet and arms. They laid her in a cart next to a wounded soldier. The cart began to move. She held her eyes open only long enough to scan the blue of the sky then turned and watched as a man bled to death beside her. She slipped out of consciousness again as the wagon took a bump and her head hit the slats.

When she awoke she was lying on a palette in a large room with white-plastered walls and a tall, timbered ceiling. At the end of each beam where it met the wall was the head of the mother goddess, carved and gilded. Windows high up at either end let in a silvery light and beneath them stood tall braziers giving off warmth. On top of each rested shallow brass bowls of medicinal herbs steeping in steaming water. The clean scent of mint and eucalyptus wafted throughout the room.

At first she thought she was dreaming and she was amongst her own dear soldiers in her sleeping hall, but no, she was one of the wounded taken to The House of Good Women, a hospital run by those who had dedicated their lives to the healing of the city's residents. There were twenty beds in the ward filled with injured and dying men and yet for the first time in many days Aolwynd smiled with gratitude and gave herself over to sleep and safety.

17

"...All in the Head."

Aolwynd was awakened by the touch of a wash cloth against her drumming forehead. The warm water wiped away the blood and soot gently from her face and she opened her eyes to see a young woman gazing back at her. The nurse smiled and lowered her head shyly as she rang out the cloth and reached out to wash Aolwynd's neck. Aolwynd grabbed her hand in panic.

"Please sir, let me just remove the blood and dirt, then you may sleep again."

Aolwynd suffered the girl to wash her neck, then clean and bandage her burnt hands one after the other.

"Thank you." Aolwynd whispered in a scorched and raspy voice, her throat raw from the smoke and fumes.

"Your hands are not calloused from heavy labor like

some or you would not have suffered as much from the fire, look at these blisters! Did you see much fighting? These are the hands of a scholar, not a warrior..."

Aolwynd smiled. "Yes, there is some truth in it, my father is a scholar."

The nurse's face lit up as she smiled still holding Aolwynd's hand. "There, I thought so. Still, you're a hero. The garrison is taken back."

"And the city?"

"They are still fighting in the east but some say it will be over soon enough. Them pirates are bein' pushed back through the streets, neighborhood by neighborhood and the East Gate is closed to them."

"Brilla! You're needed!" A woman of authority suddenly entered the ward. She was tall and dressed in a periwinkle blue gown covered by a clean white apron. Brilla dropped the bandaged hand abruptly, the color coming to her cheeks.

"Good moro, young man, how do you feel? You were lucky to escape death, apart from the crack on your skull and those burned hands. Rest. Brilla will bring you some broth later." She looked sternly at the nurse. She began to walk away but coming back she warned, "Toy with her, young buck, and I'll bring you a physic instead." With that she pulled Brilla up by the arm and sent her on to the next patient.

That night more soldiers were brought in and settled on beds emptied by the dying or on mattresses laid between the pallets on the floor. The soldiers told of a great battle to take the eastern ramparts of the city and of how it failed. The corsairs were still too many and in control of a few neighborhoods. Barricades choked the streets and fortified the whole district against assault. It was like a cage they said, holding citizens in as well as the soldiers out.

Aolwynd propped herself up on one arm to listen to an old guard.

"Aye...we'll take 'em, it's ony time in the way now tickin' off their names on the dead man's scroll, they're gettin' desperate, won't be long now."

"Can you tell me...did they rescue the Guardian's son?"

"Oh! Aye! Nah then...that's a tale ta' tell! The harbor folk started it all they say. Rose up and burned the ships! Clever that. Pushed boats inta them...all aflame! The fire burnt a warehouse or two but yah canna buy a cake at a fish stall. It didn't 'alf stink w' all them spices and stuff. Ah ony eat pepper meself. Won't be anymore o' tha' fer a while I reckon, till the trade starts up again."

"The battle?"

"Oh. Aye. They fought them devils in the streets an' charged up the hill! That were a day, eh? An' 'oo do yew think was leadin' them troops inta garrison? Jorus! By the gods! 'E's a clever 'ol fox. Must 'av slipped a band o' them guardians in somehow. E' knows 'is way about, that one. I knew 'im years back, when ah still 'ad me hair on me head an' a bone in me shaft." The old man grabbed his groin for a general laugh, enjoying his audience. "'E 'ad three widows goin' at once in three different parts o' the city...but that's a tale fer a different time." The old man coughed and hacked, having spilled all his breath. Relishing the thought of many days of their undivided attention he laid himself back down and closed his eyes.

The men laughed and murmured prayers to the Twin War Gods for the city's deliverance before they grew quiet and slept.

Aolwynd fell back on her pillow and closed her eyes. Faolan was safe...and Boru still alive and fighting somewhere.

The Matron bustled in with clean blankets. "Now then!

Quiet you lot! Go to sleep." she ordered. Women carried out basins of urine and bloody bandages and the hall went dark.

Brilla was sitting by Aolwynd's bed watching her as she woke the next morning. She inched her stool closer and felt Aolwynd's forehead. "How are thee this morning?"

"Hungry."

"Tha's a good sign. I'll be away ta' git yah some bread soaked in broth."

"Sounds awful."

"Then yer better than ye' look."

"Thanks." Aolwynd said rubbing the tender bump on her skull.

"I didna mean tha'...I mean yer a bit beaten up but I like your looks." she giggled.

"Brilla, I must tell you..."

"Oh, aye. My luck. You've a girl somewhere." She fussed with the blanket, tucking it in, bending over her hero. She smelled of soap and mint. She made to fluff the pillow but reached out and stroked Aolwynd's hair instead, pushing the fingers of one hand through the short curls. With the other hand she lifted Aolwynd's head, held it next to her heart for a fraction of a second longer than seemed necessary and resettled it on the pillow. Memories of intense intimacy awoke in Aolwynd from this warmth and she was stunned to discover a confusion of feelings. She looked up at the girl wondering, experiencing what a man must feel when a woman comes close and offers herself and her comfort.

"There...that's better. You know, you're almost as sweet as the Guardian's son."

"He's here?" Aolwynd choked out, sitting up so fast her head swam. The blood pounded against the inside of her skull. She was suddenly spinning as if she'd been thrown from a horse. Choking on her own vomit she threw up in a stream on the blanket. She crashed back down against the pillow with a mighty groan. Stars were popping behind her eyelids.

"Now see what you've done! You naughty boy!" Brilla said clicking her tongue and secretly enjoying this added time to tend to her favorite. She stripped the blanket off and replaced it with a new one, going through her enticing ritual once again. Finally wiping Aolwynd's face she laid the bandaged hands on top of the covers. "Yes...he's come around nicely, our Faolan. Wicked skinny he was but you've got to expect tha', filthy pirates...such a handsome lad, an' so obliging." She taunted Aolwynd a little. "We'll see 'im alreet agin. Now you rest, Naughty." Her cool fingertips touched Aolwynd's forehead then slid down over her eyelids forcing them to close. Aolwynd felt spellbound and fell into an uneasy sleep in which she rocked in the bottom of a sinking boat.

Two more days passed. News of the battles going street by street kept everyone on edge. Every new wounded man had a little news or a little hearsay to add. It was very close fighting now, in narrow spaces, this much they all understood, alleys and dead ends, difficult to maneuver and barely enough room to swing a blade. When the soldiers broke through one of the many barricades, the scum would haul out a captive and use them as a human shield, backing out of the skirmish and killing their victim when they left.

One morning Aolwynd awoke to find Jem sitting by her side. She lurched upwards and threw her arms about his neck. Her heart pounded and the stars returned, circling about his face as she looked long and hard at him. He laid her back down. Glancing shyly about he picked up her hand and kissed it. He held it and patted it all the while they talked.

She saw that his arm and shoulder were bandaged. "You're wounded!"

"Aye...it's a proper war wound too." he chuckled.

"You're a soldier now?"

"Pr'aps yer reet, pr'aps ah should do. Not too old ta change, eh?"

"Handsome..." she murmured, almost without thinking.

"Aye? Oh, tha's m' boy!" he said looking around furtively as The Matron passed near by.

"Have you seen Boru? Have you told him I'm alive?"

"Nay." he answered truculently. "Thar's no way ta' git through the fightin'. It's tha' thick."

"Then they think we're dead."

"Aye. Boru sent men t' harbor the day after, went round by the south end, same as we came in. That Halduro is back an' in charge o' findin' you. Well, you know 'im...'E wasna half pleased ta' find the burnt bodies amid all tha' muck. You an' me an' the pirates like, I suppose 'E thought. Didn't find the gold though. I'll go round an' poke about after a while an' see if I can dig it oop. Tak it to yer Dah an' tell 'im yer alive when they open the gates. I reckon I can git thar or sea way."

"Tell Boru, tell Faolan, please."

"I toll yer...I can't get to 'em right now. '*Yer man*'s still fightin'," he said with wicked emphasis, "an' that boy they've got here, Faolan... Halduro's got guards on 'is room, can't nobody get in there 'sept the Good Wives. 'E's a bastard, tha' general." Jem stared off into space and his eyes were dark.

Aolwynd felt a twinge of guilt and the tears welled up in her eyes, remembering all they'd been through and how much he'd done for her. "Oh Jem...I'm so glad your safe!"

"Looked all over fer you, I did. Fair frightened out of m' wits. Y'know they burned the dead right quick in a pyre by the sea. Afraid o' the pest. I was sure you were in it." He looked into her eyes and she saw there were tears in his own. Raking his hand through his black curls, he licked his lips. "Ah was near distracted. Missin' you. Don't think I'd get over it.

The old soldier next to them watched this display with interest. Especially when Jem kissed her hand again.

"What 'er yew lookin' at nobhead? Roll over an' go ta' sleep!" Jem cursed him under his breath. "Aye...then I remembered the cart for the Good Wives goin' off from the garrison. Figured, 'Why would it be there if there weren't no one left alive?' So off I flew here. Then they wouldn't let me in fer a few days...an' no one by yer name in the women's wards..." His head bent down and he stared at his hands. "Then ah remembered the haircut...seeing you...now..." he lapsed into silence.

"I really shouldn't be here, we should tell them." she whispered.

"Shhh. No. Doon't tell 'em yet. I couldna' visit if they moved you to the women's wards. Please. I want you all t' m'self fer a wee while. Is tha' so much ta' ask?" He laid his cheek against her hand. His touch was so warm. That warmth again, her brain was swimming. She closed her eyes and groaned.

"That's enoof now, father..." Brilla said coming over with a bowl of fish broth. "I'll have to ask you to leave."

Jem laughed as Aolwynd's eyes popped open.

"Uncle, brother, father, only close relatives, you know the rules."

"Aye, broother then, or maybe somethin' like." he whispered in her ear as he stood up, his face passing close to Aolwynd's. "I'll tell Mam yer alreet." He called out,

205

leaving.

"Well, he seems very fond of you." Brilla purred as she tried to force some foul broth into Aolwynd's closed mouth.

The old man in the next bed coughed and rolled back over onto his elbow staring at Aolwynd. He made a little kiss with his lips. Aolwynd glared at him.

Brilla fed her more broth. Aolwynd complained bitterly that it needed seasoning and salt.

"An joost whar' are we supposed to get that with the Spice Man's warehouse burned to the ground? Complainin'? Then I think it's time you had a wash an' got into this nice clean bed shirt. Even ol' Scruffy there 'as 'ad a wash." Brilla said jerking her head at the old man.

"Aye! Do tha' agin any time y'like beautiful!"

Brilla ignored him, pointing to the folded garment at the foot of Aolwynd's bed. She reached for Aolwynd's collar.

Again Aolwynd grabbed her hand. "No." she said huskily.

"If you won't do it, I'll get help."

"Try it."

"Reet. Stay like a pig in the mook then. I'll no be kissin' yew! I'm through playin'. We've 'ad trooble with the young lord today too. He keeps wantin' ta visit the women's wards. Claims 'E's lookin' fer someone. Little devil. Yer' all gettin' better an' that's fer sure. Things are stirrin'."

"Who is he looking for?"

"Soom one 'E wants ta thank. 'E's fair determined. But we've women in labor in those wards. No men allowed! That's all they need is some man faffin' about in there. They don't want ta be seen when they're not pretty! What woman does?" Brilla smoothed out her apron front and smelled a sprig of blue flowers she had pinned to the bodice.

Aolwynd could tell she was waiting for a compliment. 'I'd have tried that when I was sixteen.' she thought. That mischievous confusion came over her again and to her shame and pleasure she felt strangely flirtatious. Aolwynd toyed with the silly girl, enjoying the feeling of being in control of someone. "The flower matches your eyes. Let me smell." she whispered. To her delight Brilla leaned nearer. Aolwynd hooked a finger in the shoulder strap of the nurse's apron and pulled her close, holding her there to smell the flower.

Brilla was trembling. Her cheeks reddened prettily and she lowered her lashes, looking at the hand near her bosom. Aolwynd couldn't help grinning. She remembered doing a lot of that as she grew into womanhood, astonished at her own body and its changes. She suddenly felt very fond of this girl and ashamed of herself for tricking her. But she also wondered if learning about love and how to love left you open to experiencing all its forms...she'd never given it a thought before, so obsessed she'd been with Boru, her exploration of her own body and his.

Her headache returned with a vengeance. "I'm too sensible for all this. My skull must be cracked, idiot thoughts are seeping out!" she mumbled. "Maybe this is all in my head."

"Eh?" Brilla said pushing her gently back down on the pillow. She pursed her lips together and shook her head smiling, as if chastening a mischievous child. "Ahm no dream...Ahm' yer best dream..." she whispered.

Was it Aolwynd's imagination or was the young nurse skipping as she left the room. She *was* swinging the slop bucket.

Aolwynd lay back with her hands behind her head staring at the ceiling. The carved face of a goddess above her looked 'just like Brilla'. she thought.

The old soldier next to her was sitting upright in his bed gawping at her, his jaw slack with a look of complete confusion on his face. 'Me too.' she thought shooting him a grin and closing her eyes.

That night there were tales of a great battle fought in the eastern marketplace, a last stand by the corsairs near the very place Boru and she had passed through so long ago to rescue her father.

The troops had opened the gate from the plains beyond the city and flooded the streets with soldiers heading toward the market. The pirates went to their deaths with their backs against the wall. Many soldiers also died or were injured. The Good Women flew about the ward already choked with soldiers, making ready, opening another hall, moving mattresses and spreading blankets on the floor.

When the women were finished, they took their lanterns away and only the light from the braziers lit the ward. Aolwynd sat up and put her feet on the floor. Waiting a moment for the room to stop spinning, she tried to remember where the stairs to the upper levels were. She knew there were private chambers above her and that is where they would have put Lord Borchard's son. Aolwynd tip-toed past the staff rooms and climbed a flight, shakily holding onto the railing. At the end of a long hallway she saw a guard sitting at a table. One candle illumined the darkness.

She made no noise and slipped along the dark passage toward the dozing guard. Of a sudden he stood up and walked out of his circle of light toward the opposite staircase. Light came up through the rungs growing brighter and brighter. A Good Woman with a lantern was followed by another carrying a tray of food for the guard. He made small talk for a moment and as he did so Aolwynd slipped inside the room.

An oil lamp burned on a stand near a comfortable bed. She walked up to it and her shadow fell across Faolan's face. He looked thin and drawn, his lips were chapped and he surely had been beaten for traces of bruising were still present about his face. Tears caught in her throat. He opened his eyes, startled, as if ready to fend someone off. She held him down and in an instant he recognized her. His face showed wonder and surprise but most of all happiness. There was the boy she knew, still there in spite of everything. He held up his arms and they embraced.

"It's you! It's really you!" he whispered, touching her cropped hair. "I thought you were dead. You're not a dream are you?"

"I'm real enough."

"You can't be found here. The guards have been told to kill anyone who tries to enter. Halduro is so pleased you are dead. He'll hang you if he gets the chance, it's what he planned to do all along."

"Tell your brother I'm alive."

"Thank the Twins you came tonight! I'm well enough to leave tomorrow and the way is safe now. We'd have never known." He gazed warmly at her holding her hand. "Thank you for saving me...and your father...give him my thanks as well. I'm so ashamed. Tell me...what happened to Fila? No one will say and I need to know."

Aolwynd told him of her death and of their last meeting, of Gerda's forgiveness and love for the girl and that she passed peacefully. He stared at the ceiling while she recounted all that had happened. His eyes were black in the dark room and glistened with tears.

18

Warriors and Givers of Life

"Sleep now." she said as she blew him a kiss and crept softly to the door. The guard was snoring heavily. She slipped along the wall and back down the stairs, hanging onto the banister trying to fight off the dizziness that was coming over her. She just made it back to her pallet without passing out.

All was quiet in the ward. The bed next to hers was empty. A man had died in it earlier and they had not yet replaced him. 'Old Scruffy' on her other side made only the sound of shallow, raspy breathing.

Aolwynd closed her eyes and fell asleep. In what seemed like an instant she felt soft lips upon her own. Aolwyn sleepily returned the kiss. It was dark in the hall but for the brazier of glowing coals. Opening her eyes she could see Brilla's shining eyes and feel the closeness of her warm body hovering over her. The girl let her apron fall to the floor and loosened the front of her gown. Suddenly she lifted the blanket and climbed on top of Aolwynd, straddling her hips. Leaning in, she kissed her face and neck swaddling the covers about them both. Aolwynd grabbed her about the waist. Brila groaned and held her hands there, forcing the embrace, not letting go.

"Brilla, stop!"

The girl sighed happily. Tucking the blanket beneath Aolwyn's shoulders she snaked her hands up to Aolwynd's face. She shook her by the ears gently with an affectionate movement as if she were grasping a puppy's head. "It's allreet, they won't be comin' in fer a while yet. Let's pretend we're not here, an' we're all alone."

Dizzy from Brilla's playfulness Aolwynd tried to stay alert. "No...I mean...you see..."

Aolwynd struggled free and grabbed her by the wrists. "By the Gods, Brilla! I'm not..." she gasped for air trying not to shout and wake the whole ward. Brilla's stare was sultry.

"Take me sweet heart...ah kin see yer ready, let's see what you've got fer me."

She let out a shriek. "You bitch!" she cried.

Brilla, shocked and not thinking, hit her in the face, then rolled off the bed, dragging the covers with her to the floor. "Help! Sisters! Cere! Lyla!" Brilla yelled as she ran from the ward. The wounded men were startled, woke, called out and groaned. Some men tried to get up, thinking they were under attack.

When the Good Women came running Aolwynd pretended to be unconscious. It seemed the best thing to do. As they gathered around, Brilla blathered some tale through her tears about the soldier being out of his head and how she was going to take the opportunity to get him 'out of 'is stinking clothes and into a nice clean night shirt even though it wasn't bath time and wasn't this a nasty business, she discovered, him not bein' a man at all!'

The Matron strode in and with a flick of her finger sent Brilla out of the room. This wasn't the first time the girl had been caught with a lover. Cere and Lyla only laughed at first then scowled their disapproval. Making eyes, they whispered remarks to each other and picking up the girl's apron from the floor, told the men to go back to sleep.

Aolwynd kept her eyes shut tight and groaned dramatically as they transferred her to a stretcher and carried her out.

It was quiet and peaceful in the Women's Ward with the soft snoring of pregnant women accompanied by the occasional snort. One small light illuminated the humps and bumps of rounded women's bodies. Aolwynd was put in a corner bed with a screen around it.

Brilla came to tuck her in and see that she was settled. "Matron's revenge..." she grumbled. "'yer my patient now. Ere, ah'll finally get tha' filthy clothing off yah and wash away the dirt, tha's summit, I guess. Or maybe it were Cere an' Lyla's idea...them two women live together ya' know. Wouldn't put it past 'em. They're laughin' at me now, I just know it."

"I tried to tell you."

"Bitch." Brilla whispered crossly. "My hero!" she sighed helping her charge into bed. "I'm sorry about the clout. Thanks fer not sayin' noothin'. Tha' would a' cost me my position. I been warned 'afore, y'know. It woulda' served me right, w' my reputation, getting' tossed out fer fookin' a girl."

Aolwynd sat up on one elbow and put her hand over her

heart. She bowed her head like a courtier. "My lady." she said smiling wickedly.

"Good the Gods!" Brilla cursed softly, pushing Aolwynd back on the pillow. "You're *terrible!*" She turned on her heels and flounced away with a smile.

The women's ward was boring but much more luxurious than the men's. There were tall windows that reached to the floor and opened out onto a grand balcony overlooking the sea. Couches with pillows lay waiting for expectant mothers to recline and take their ease in the sun. Tall palms and pots of flowers were everywhere affording them color and privacy.

The Matron visited each morning, stopping to chat with every patient. Her smile and kind concern was evident, in contrast, her demeanor in the men's wards was much more brusque and business-like. Aolwynd watched her from a comfortable lounge outside, near the balustrade. The sun was pouring strength back into her and she stretch her arms like a cat. Sea gulls called from above, their white wings piercing the air.

Lauro, head of the order of Good Women came over to Aolwynd last of all her patients and sat down at her feet gazing out over the water. "And how is our young buck today?"

Aolwynd smiled sheepishly and coughed, covering her mouth as she did so.

The Matron chuckled. "I did warn you about Brilla. You should have told us...why did you not?"

"Truly I could not think clearly and then..."

"Ah...your friend. You did it for your brother? So you could see him? Perhaps Brilla would be better for you after all." she teased.

Aolwynd took her joke as intended. "No. Sweet as she is

I love another."

"Too bad. She's a good girl but needs to marry."

"And soon!"

The Matron laughed. "I would say you suffer from the same hot blood as she and I know who stirs it. But I think you have a better chance of marrying Brilla than the one you love...I know who he is. I'm sorry for you. You have risked everything for our city...no...our country, and for the Supreme Guardian, or was it only for his son that you've done all this? Anyway, much good it will do you. No favor...as they say, goes unpunished."

"Tell me something..." Aolwynd asked as her hands were un-bandaged and examined.

"If I can..."

"The men's wards...are so plain, oh, not lacking anything but..." Aolwynd raised her arm and gestured about her.

"Ah...I do what I can for Warriors, and we call all men that. Their needs are different, their desires are base. They cut through their lives and their families like a blade. But for The Bringers of Life...nothing is too good." She trailed off into a reverie of her own looking out at the sea. "Women are sacred here, every one of them, rich and poor alike, all have the power of life given to them by the Great Mother. Men only have the power of death. We are on a higher plane and should be treated like queens yet we so seldom are. That's why I spoil them. Men are base."

Aolwynd puffed out her cheeks.

"You may think what you like...I have my reasons." She examined Aolwynd's burnt hands. "Hold your palms up to the sun, it will help to heal them."

The Matron rose and smoothed her gown. Leaning on the balustrade she suddenly turned and looked at Aolwynd with the eyes of a bird of prey. "You would be welcome here, you know...why not join us? You have proved your courage...and your curiosity." Her eyes were full of merriment. "You have the quick wit of a scholar and nothing frightens you. I could teach you to heal, how to cut open a living body...remove disease and fix what is broken. Why spend your life running an inn...or following an army? There are many secrets I could teach you."

Aolwynd no longer saw the bustling matron, lugging blankets and carrying away bed pans but who she really was, a brave and learned doctor standing before her, powerful and full of mysteries. "Thank you, but my path is still unclear to me." Aolwynd said studying the white caps and trying to rise from her couch.

"Stay. Rest yourself. Come back to us when it is your time at least. We will see his child safely born. That much we can do for you."

Aolwynd stopped what she was doing with her mouth hanging open. The wind picked up suddenly as she fell backwards upon the couch. When she looked up The Matron was gone.

On the narrow drive below the balcony a cart pulled up to the hospice followed by Halduro riding his horse. The Matron appeared at the entrance as he came up the wide sandstone steps. A cold wind blew. His feet crunched the dead fronds of the palm trees that lined the staircase.

He bowed formally and smiled his courtier's smile, only his eyes remained cold. "Lauro, how nice to see you again, beautiful as ever."

"Hal. I heard you had been killed." she said without expression.

"Not yet, my dove." he said with a knowing smile. "I have come to collect my charge. He has been treated royally, I am sure. But the siege is over and his father is anxious for his return."

"As I would be if he were my son."

Haldoro looked into Lauro's eyes and his smile faded away. Coming up onto the same step as she, he leaned into her ear. "What is past is past. Let us be friends, if we can."

She pulled her hand ever so slowly out of his grasp as if from the hole of some vermin that might strike at any moment. Halduro followed her into the building and up the stairs to Faolan's room.

She stood like stone in the doorway as he passed. "He would have been mine if you had not poisoned Borchard against me."

"It was over long ago. Forget him." Halduro hissed as he walked into the room.

Aolwynd watched from the veranda as two soldiers soon carried Faolan out on a stretcher. Halduro and Lauro followed. It took but a moment to settle him in the cart. Halduro made to shake The Matron's hand before he mounted his horse but she did not take it.

"Faolan will tell him...and he'll come for me. I'm alive my love, and your child with me." Aolwynd whispered and sank back onto her pillow.

19

Dark Arts

A night and a day went by and Aolwynd was still
waiting to see her captain. Her heart expected, in fact
envisioned him riding in through the gate of her inn then
driving his horse up the steps of the hospital, looking
feverishly for her, finally charging into the Women's Ward
sweeping her into his arms and carrying her away. Beyond
that she did not think nor care.

But he did not come.

Brilla scolded her for not eating, touching nothing at the
women's dining table. By now, everyone was aware of who
she was, what she had done and tragically, whom she
loved. The other patients patted her hand and murmured
excuses for him but all agreed privately that she was just
one more abandoned woman. The Matron stared at her with

an amused expression, like a specimen in a bottle.

Brilla coaxed and coddled but Aolwynd lay on her bed all day with her face to the wall. Finally the windows were closed and a candle lit for the night. "Coom on Sweeting...eat summit. It's gettin' cold. I've got to tak anoother tray somewhere after this. I'll never be finished tonight if yah doon't eat." Finally even Brilla's patience wore out. "Suit yerself." she sighed and left.

One by one the women stopped their chatter and fell asleep. The hours passed by as Aolwynd stared at the ceiling. A shadow flitted across it and an excited Brilla slipped behind the screen. "Coom on!" she whispered spitting in Aolwynd's ear, grabbing her by the arm and throwing back the blanket.

"No..." Aolwynd moaned.

"Coom on! I've got summit ta show thee! Coom with me now!" Brilla growled and dragged her out of bed.

Down the dark hallway they tip-toed to a part of the building Aolwynd had never seen before, a wing that stood apart from the others. They passed through a vast airy room that seemed to be all windows. It jutted out onto a promontory of rock above the sea so that it was filled with light by day yet was still very private, removed from the rest of the hospital. Only the roar of the waves could be heard all around them, blocking out distraction. Aolwynd had often wondered what went on inside this structure as she peered at it from her couch on the balcony.

In the center of the room was a long wooden table the top of which was completely enveloped in metal. Knives and instruments of all kinds were arranged on countertops. Bandages and towels lay stacked on shelves. In one corner a large copper kettle as big as a barrel fashioned with a spigot stood above a brazier.

"Lauro's Surgery." Brilla whispered.

They left it and passed into a narrow corridor. Brilla hesitated beside one of many doors then peeped her head in and disappeared inside. She reached back out for Aolwynd's hand and pulled her in. Brilla put a finger to her lips. "There's a guard asleep outside t'other door, so be quiet. They joost brought 'im in this aft'. She's only just finished takin' the metal out of 'im. Doon't mak' no noise...Ahm' trustin' yah. I'll be back."

Aolwynd's eyes filled with tears and her heart began to pound before she even entered. There in the dark room lay Boru. A small brazier stood beside him steaming herbs. His right arm and chest were tightly bandaged. It seemed so long since she had seen him, she crept close, afraid to wake him, afraid to touch him. Just to see him again was proof enough that heaven existed. 'This man, was it this man, who knew me so intimately, so much better than I knew my own flesh, my very self?' she choked quietly with emotion. He was like a stranger lying there, she did not know what to do.

"Who is there?" he whispered groggily, opening his eyes. "Matron? Is that you?"

"No..." was all Aolwynd managed to say.

He turned his head and in the dim light of the coals, squinted, trying to make out her form. "Boy? Water, please."

She brought a cup to his lips and held the nape of his neck as he tried to drink. She kissed his temple before letting his head drop gently back onto the pillow.

He grabbed the hand that held the cup. "Who are you? Why do you touch me?"

"Aolwynd...it's Aolwynd." she whispered.

His eyes grew wild with pain. "No...she's dead! Don't torture me! Who sent you? Halduro? To mock me? Curse you! Jorus gave me her letter...Halduro found the bodies...he swore..."

"Halduro lied. I'm here my love."

"The drugs...what's happening...I'm dreaming."

"You are not." She stroked his cheek and kissed him. His lips were bitter from the sleeping draught Lauro had given him.

Hurried footsteps came back along the Surgery corridor. Brilla popped her head in the door.

"Soom one's on the way...ye' 'av ta go now!"

"I'll be back." Aolwynd breathed in his ear. His hand reached out into the darkness after her.

Halduro's voice, the sound of footsteps and angry conversation approaching fast carried down the outer hallway. Aolwynd had just time enough to slip away. Brilla dragged her all the way back to the ward and held her as she cried.

As Halduro walked into the small recovery room he was assaulted by the smell of healing herbs. He waved his hand in front of his face and smiled as he lit another candle. "The sooner you're out of this place the better, I swear. Witches." he scowled dramatically, looked about the room, then sighed. "How does our hero?"

Boru stared at him as if he were an insect, then considering, he sat up. "My brother. How is he?"

"Always the brother comes first...he is stronger every day. He is young."

"Have you anything to report?" Boru said coldly.

"Ah...don't be like that...you have won a great victory my lad...saved your first city. You can ride home in triumph, and to great celebrations I'm told."

"Save your sweet words for someone who believes them. How are my men? Are there any still within these walls? How many died in the last battle?"

"Calm yourself. All is well. We're still cleaning up the pirate dead, burning their bodies with the siege towers, tidying up, as it were, making ready to leave. Your men are busy helping the citizens resettle...Tanner has taken charge of that...those that still have homes to go to."

"Has there been any word...of her?"

"Nothing. I told you, she is dead." Halduro lowered his voice in mock sympathy but with the finality of a closed door.

Boru sank down into his pillow and shut his eyes. "I had a dream...it was her and yet not her...she seemed so real...she came to me, here...and spoke her name." He pulled his hand across his damp forehead and covered his eyes.

"I would have you be wary, my friend, you have been injured, and are weak...there are things here...Lauro has knowledge of the ancient arts...this whole house with its potions...the goddess they worship here has her purposes, things may not be what they seem...or they may be more than they seem."

At that moment Lauro walked in. "Dreams you say? Our guests have lots of funny dreams when they are coming out of my surgery, my preparations take away the pain but they are strong and befuddle the mind sometimes. What did you dream?"

"It was nothing." the two men said in unison.

Halduro smiled his secretive smile and bowed to the doctor. "Our illustrious surgeon is right. Pay it no attention." He called over his shoulder as he left the room. "You will soon be shed of this place and this city. I'll be back, you're looking well. I will send word to your father that we only wait on your orders, ready to march."

Lauro took hold of Boru's wrist and felt his pulse. "Warm and steady. So, you will leave the city?"

"We are finished here." he sighed.

"I hear we are to congratulate you, you have a bride waiting on your return to the capitol, and from a great family."

"So it would seem."

"You are not anxious for this to happen? Forgive me if I pry."

"Yes, I mean no, I am not willing for this to happen..."

"But?"

"I love another...I loved another...she is dead."

"I am sorry. I gave up helping sweethearts long ago. I have no preparations that will mend a broken heart. I wish I did. I would have used them on myself." she sighed and smiled. "But time and occupation can also heal."

"Healing others?"

"Yes, or serving one's country." She felt his forehead. "Cool. That is good. I will order you some food and change that bandage later." Her voice trailed off as she opened the door to leave. "Try to sleep, my son."

She was deep in thought as she stepped out into the hallway. Halduro grasped her arm and drew her quickly aside, forcing her back against a wall of windows. "I'm taking him out of here...prepare him to leave."

"Still listening at key holes, Hal? He needs rest, at least a few days for that wound to the chest."

"He needs to be away from you and your women!" Halduro turned, looking out over the grounds, still holding her and digging his fingers into her arm. In the silver moonlight the herb gardens picked out tessellated patterns across the grass.

"You and your fancies of a life that never happened!" he said in a low voice. "And now that whore...how did she ever find him?" he turned. "I know she's here, somewhere in this cursed place, you're hiding her...you found her and

224

patched her up, she spoke with Faolan though I set my own guards to protect him. How did that happen? She is a criminal! This hospice! This place I built for you! Our bargain long ago! Your silence...your consent and Borchard's free of you. It has all been a very bad bargain for me."

"You're a monster." She said through clenched teeth. "How is it you're still alive? I hear he almost killed you once..." she motioned to Boru's door with a grimace. "but then, I fear there is too much poison in you to die."

He sneered at her. "Prepare him. Do not let me hear you call him 'son' again. Your son is dead. You had no son. That was our bargain. Borchard will never know of him. You agreed to that. I protect the realm. Me! If you speak of this again, to any one, I will ruin you and all that you have built here. I will have you and your Good Women burned in front of your hospital for the witches that you are! You run perilously close to offending the gods with your dark arts. I know you cut open the living and the dead! You go far beyond what you have been taught! You offend the goddess! This is devil's work!"

Lauro glared at him and grinned with solemn eyes. "I loved him."

"Your family was nothing."

"He loved me."

"Don't fool yourself," Halduro strode down the hall then stopped and turned, "and be ready to do me one more favor."

A tear fell from Lauro's eye. She rubbed the bruises blooming on her arm where he held her throughout the whole of their conversation. She walked slowly down some stairs and out a door into the garden.

20

Three Little Graves

The lawns surrounding the hospital were full of fruit trees and medicinal plants in small beds. The trees, heavy with each kind of fruit sheltered benches where women patients could sit and rest themselves. The 'Warriors' were allowed no such luxury. Pathways lined with berry bushes and flowerbeds lead to the vegetable gardens. Lauro sat on a bench until dawn, the hem of her gown soaking up the dew. A blue trail spiraled about on the grass where she had walked away the night. She stood up and made her way to a tall hedge of cypresses. A gate of iron squealed as she opened it and passed through to a private place. Set into a manicured lawn in neat rows, were tiny stone markers, some shaped like little lambs, others plain and unadorned. Some graves had names carved into them, others were smooth and blank. Lauro stood beside a tiny marble lamb staring down at it for a long time.

The sun was high the next day and Aolwynd had not slept. She paced the floor of her room off the veranda frantic with worry. Lauro had removed her to a small private place because the women of the ward were increasingly upset by her tears and remonstrances.

Brilla found her talking loudly to herself and staring out the window. "Coom on, it's time ta' wash." She carried in a basin of hot water that smelled of soap and lavender. Over her arm she carried a towel. "This should soothe yah, just smell it."

"Thank you, I'll do it myself...leave me alone..." Aolwynd was sharp, then remembering her manners, "if you please, my lady." she said more softly, relieving Brilla of her burden and setting it down on a stand. Brilla batted her eyes and pouted, trying to make her laugh, then left the room.

Aolwynd moved the stand into the sunlight and unbuttoning her shift, letting it fall to the waist. She dipped the sponge into the soapy water. It felt deliciously warm and slippery against her skin.

The afternoon sun shone on her wet shoulders. The door to her room opened quietly and closed softly.

"Do my back as long as you're here." she teased and held up the sponge. It was taken from her hand which made her laugh. She felt it stroking her back tenderly, then a hand massaged her neck. She sighed, near tears, but finally began to relax. "You do wonderful work here, my love, really. I cannot fault you." A man's strong arms slid about her waist and held her tightly. Aolwynd gasped. She reached up behind her head to hold his neck and his mouth pressed against her shoulder. "My love..." she sighed, hoping against hope, spellbound. Jem turned her slowly around and covered her mouth with his. The taste of the sea was on his lips. Her eyes opened wide.

"Please..." he whispered, his eyes glistening, "just for once, pretend tha' you love me." Jem picked her up and carried her to the bed.

Instinctively Aolwynd curled into a ball and turned away from him, sobbing as she did so.

Aolwynd was still lying down at suppertime. Her face was to the wall and she was staring at her index finger as it traced the pattern of leaves on waning sunlight coming through the window.

Jem had gone.

"Cover up, yah hussy! Who wants t' see tha'? Just look at yersel!" Brilla walked in and flipped the blanket overAolwynd's exposed back side. "I've a message fer yah. An' it's suppertime. You'll be eatin' with the ladies, if yer not too good fer 'em."

"What?" Aolwynd said, clearing her throat.

"I said...I've a message."

"What is it?"

"What's this...yer shift? Argh...look at this mess." Brilla picked up the wet garment and the towel from the floor. "Soom one don't care what I have t'do...or soomone's bin 'ere. Was it Jem?"

"Yes."

Brilla stared at her and for the first time Aolwynd saw the sorrow in her friend's eyes, but it was quickly hidden. "Well, ah knew it weren't the other. Look here...you can't just lead a good man on like tha'...Great Moother! Pick one, will yah? I thought you were strong! Here you are gettin' passed from man ta man like a common basket! Make up yer damned mind!" Brilla threw the wet shift at her. It landed against the wall and slid down to the floor. "Pick up yer own mess! Ahv' got no one, me! It ain't fair. I'd give anythin'..." she mumbled staring out the window. Finally turning and rubbing her eyes she said, "I'm away now ta git yah some dry clothes. It's time you were gone from this place. Doon't go out in the hall in yer skin like tha'. Can I trust yah?"

"My message?"

"Oh, aye. the oother man." Brilla threw her a bit of paper.

Aolwynd flipped it open, it read:

"Come to me tonight. B."

She slipped down the hallway as soon as it was dark trying not to make a sound. Only the occasional candle from an open doorway flickered as she passed by. It took some minutes to find the surgical wing as Brilla would not take her. The room with the tall windows was bathed in moonlight. Everything was bleached so bright she had to shade her eyes. She found the door to the recovery rooms and after so much light it was utterly dark. She felt her way along the wall and tapped on the door.

"Come in." a voice answered her.

She stepped into the dim room illuminated by a single candle. The bed was empty and stripped of its sheets.

Halduro stepped out of the shadows. "Thank you for coming...my dear."

"Where is he?"

"Out of harm's way."

"By that you mean me." she said turning to leave.

Halduro grabbed her wrist. "Not so fast, my little cat. I've a few words of advice for you. Take them and all will be forgiven. Drop one mouse and pick up another...marry your fisherman. Yes, you're both alive...my mistake." he laughed ruefully. "Forget those who stand above you. How many times must I say this?" he mused. "My life has been full of foolish women trying to climb higher than is good for them!"

"Let go of me!" Aolwynd snapped.

He refused and held both her wrists, leaning into her face and sneering. "I won't let you destroy the house I so carefully built!"

"You built?"

"For the last time, I'm warning you. We'll be gone from this fish market in a matter of days. I will tell The Guardian to drop the charges against you and your family when he comes...oh yes, he is coming, my love...there is still the trial hanging over your pretty shorn head. How is that for mercy, eh? Think on it. I stand between you and the hangman. Is it not rich? Do we have a bargain here? Think of your old father in prison if you care nothing for yourself. You saved him from pirates, will you not save him from spending his last days in prison? All I'm asking is that you disappear for a few days, until we're gone. Take your claws out of Boru. Let us be away with an end to this folly and let him forget you."

"Never! Faolan will tell him I'm alive. Even as we speak he may be telling him! He will come for me! I'll never desert him...I'm carrying his child!"

At that Halduro's demeanor changed. His eyes narrowed and grew dark. He cupped his hand over her mouth and dragging her to the surgery door, locked it. "Well, that bit of news was better left unsaid." he whispered.

Aolwynd bit his hand. He yelped and let go, knocking over the brazier. The basin fell to the floor with a clang. Aolwynd slipped on its contents of water and sodden herbs and fell. Halduro picked her up and dragged her over to the bed. Leaning on top of her he grabbed a pillow and pushed it down over her face. She fought, slipping and kicking out at him, reaching blindly in the air for anything to hold onto. She could not escape from beneath him.

Halduro heard the click of the door and looked up.

Lauro walked calmly in from the outer hallway carrying a stretcher. She set it down and stood next to him.

"Ah...just in time, I'm nearly finished." he wheezed, holding the pillow, pinning Aolwynd's flailing arms with difficulty. Her struggle was getting weaker, her strength almost gone.

Lauro watched without expression as Halduro's enjoyment of his task reached its peak. "The warrior relishes killing whether the cause be good or evil..." she said softly.

"What?" he asked, wrestling with his victim.

"A line from a poem...if you like."

The grin froze on his face as Lauro pulled a scalpel from her apron pocket and still without emotion plunged it deep into his side. He wheeled around with a scream of pain and disbelief. Crashing against the bed frame he held on with one hand as his body twisted and fell, his other hand still holding the pillow.

Aolwynd sat bolt upright, mouth gaping, gasping for air, like the dead come back to life.

Lauro bent down beside the man and whispered in his ear. "Did you think...Warrior...that I would let you kill a Bringer of Life? One that might have brought my own grandchild into this world?" Smiling, she drove the blade deeper into his chest, making sure, with her surgical precision that it reached the heart between the ribs. He rolled over, lifeless, air seeping from his lungs.

Three figures carrying a stretcher made a ghostly procession along the cypresses of Lauro's garden. The moon washed over the pale lawns as they appeared and disappeared snaking beneath the shadows where they could. The smallest figure went ahead with a lantern and opened the iron gate while the other two grappled with their burden. Walking carefully around the tiny headstones they laid down the stretcher carrying the body of Halduro.

"Go to the shed and bring us back two shovels." Lauro whispered. "There's a good girl."

"How can I thank you?" Aolwynd said catching her breath. Her legs shook with exertion and she wanted nothing more than to collapse upon the wet ground.

"I should have killed him years ago. How many lives would have been different had I the courage to do so." Lauro said coldly.

Brilla came back with the tools. "'Ere, why don't we joost chuck 'im off the cliff an' let the sea tak 'im?"

"Because the sea is a fickle accomplice, my dear and cannot be trusted. I've seen her play with things for days along the shore. He must disappear, as he had planned for me so long ago, as he had planned for you." she looked at Aolwynd.

"Bastard." Brilla spat on the ground.

"Now we must cut and save the turf. We're going to make it look as if three new little graves are here instead of one long one and we need the turf for that. I only pray my little boy will not complain to the gods that he must spend eternity with an evil man lying beside him."

Aolwynd reached out to touch Lauro's shoulder but she turned away, taking the knife out of her pocket.

"A fitting tool to dig his grave. I'll bury it with him."

The women took turns first cutting the turf and rolling it aside, then digging the hole.

The sky was the color of pearls and the birds were chirping when they had finished their task. Brilla pounded the turf along its edges and feathered the blades of grass with her fingers until it looked like three little graves instead of one. Temporary wooden markers were placed at each head in place of stones as was the custom. Then they walked back together in silence.

21

Fashioning a Noose

Aolwynd slept late and when she awoke every bone
ached with exhaustion. Jem was sitting quietly with a guilty
expression on his face, his hands on his knees, looking out
the window at the sea. He lowered his head and stared at
the floor. She suddenly realized how handsome he was with
his black curly hair falling about his face and his dark eyes
under straight brows. He looked up at her and smiled
sheepishly.

"Ahm' that sorry I wasn't here to protect you last night.
Brilla told me all ye' went through...If I'd known tha'
bastard was here..." He looked down at the floor again, his
brows furrowed.

"How could you have known?"

"An' yesterday, I forced meself on you. That wasn't

right...I 'av'nt no right."

"Jem..." she said, throwing her legs over the side of the bed and trying to stand up.

He rushed over and caught her in his arms as she fell.

"You are so good to me, I don't deserve you." she breathed in his ear, her hand stroking his cheek.

"Now that's a pretty picture and no mistake." Brilla pronounced bitterly as she came in with a tray.

Lauro rushed in behind her.

"We must get her out of here! Soldiers are coming, looking for Halduro! If they find her here they will piece things together. Her charges are still in place, they will only remember the kidnapping, her pardon was all on Halduro's word and they know nothing of that! I doubt he broached it with the Guardian at all. I knew him well. Jem, you must take her away this minute. Outriders are already approaching the city gates. Take my cloak." Jem grabbed it as it was thrown and wrapped it about Aolwynd.

Brilla lead them down flight after flight of garden steps till they came out on the seaward side of the cliffs. Down a stone path they rushed, Jem carrying Aolwynd all the way to the cobblestones of the city streets below.

"Wait here." Brilla said running off.

The cold wind from the harbor set the palm trees in motion, Aolwynd shivered in her night shift, her knees shaking. Jem kept the cloak tight around her while holding her upright.

Grey storm clouds were gathering in the west. Sea gulls whirled about looking for safe haven.

Brilla came back leading a horse. She handed the reins to Jem.

"Why're folks always giv'n me a horse?" he remarked.

Brilla began to wail and threw her arms about his neck much to his surprise. He passed her over to Aolwynd.

"Dry your eyes, my lady." Aolwynd whispered in a weak voice. "We will meet again. You have been a good friend to me."

"Aye, friend? I'll always be tha', no matter what." Brilla whispered in her ear and tugged at her collar for emphasis then she kissed her cheek.

Jem lifted Aolwynd into the saddle and swung up behind her.

As they rode off, Brilla stood watching Jem curl his arms around the woman he loved. The wind blew in from the sea and Brilla hugged herself imagining his arms keeping her warm and safe, holding her tight. "What good is dreamin'..." she said turning away.

The screams of women brought her to her senses and as she ran up the stairs she saw soldiers dashing about the grounds. The hospital hallways were full of armed men. In all the wards those patients that could stand were forced up against the walls while soldiers searched the rooms.

Boru stood in Lauro's office waiting impatiently, staring out her window at the gardens. He watched as two guards brought her out from behind the cypress hedge and the iron gate. She walked toward the building with her head held high. In her hand was a watering can. After a moment she came into the room accompanied by the guards.

Boru cleared his throat and spoke. "My general did not return last night, do you know anything about this?"

Lauro merely smiled.

"And I know Aolwynd is here somewhere, alive. Bring her to me."

"Not a dream then? Please...sit down." Lauro walked proudly around her desk, in control, extending her hand as if he were a guest.

He remained standing and leaned over her as she began

shuffling and organizing her papers. He slammed his hand down on top of them. "Have you seen him?"

Lauro sighed. "Not since the afternoon he came to take you away, much to my displeasure. How is your shoulder? Do you have full movement yet? Have you any pain? It cannot yet be fully healed." Boru glared at her without answering. "Ah well, you know, he did not confide in me. We have not been friends for a long time. And even though you have returned us our city, it has never been a safe place to walk after nightfall, pirates or no pirates."

He paced the floor and went back to the window. "Where is Aolwynd?"

"Perhaps she has gone home, she was well enough."

Boru released the guards with a wave of his hand and closed the door.

"You have lied to me on every count."

"Not lied...a doctor hesitates to act you know, unless the way is clear."

"Are you sure he did not harm her? He wanted her dead."

"Yes, and I heard you nearly killed him once defending her. Happy prospect, long delayed." Boru studied her face but there was only the hint of a smile. "I know she is safe. Her sweetheart will see to that."

He whipped around and stared at her. Now it was her turn to watch for a reaction. "Sweetheart?" His face registered confusion as she spoke, then his eyes became dark, his brow furrowed and the corners of his mouth drew down.

"Yes, the fisherman. He has been very attentive." She glanced nonchalantly at her paperwork. "Here every day. We allowed him to visit. Made an exception. So gentle with her...perhaps there is more than one kind of man after all...let me think, when I have time, perhaps I will change my mind about things, not a warrior like you, certainly. Ask Brilla, she knows."

Boru grasped the hilt of his sword unconsciously as if for support. "Why do you say these things to me? You must know who she is...what she has done for my sake...how much I love her...what she means to me?"

"I say these things only to give you pause, my lord, to make you think what might be best for her. You have surely had these thoughts yourself? Otherwise you would have defied your father long ago. What would you do? Would you keep her? Drag her from campaign to campaign, something slightly less than those bedraggled soldier's wives I have seen...sorry, worried and always hungry? Little more than a camp follower, perhaps better dressed." she allowed herself a smirk. "Hasn't she fallen far enough for you yet? Your father would never allow the marriage. You are too important a playing piece for his game of realms and alliances. Nor would he let you bring her into the Guardian's Palace as a concubine even if the cloud of Halduro's disappearance and your brother's kidnapping did not hang over her."

Boru set his teeth with disgust but also a guilty sense of the truth of her words washed over him, mad though she appeared to be. Finally he said, "So you admit that Halduro is dead?" He opened the door and motioned for the guards to come back in.

"I admit nothing, but I think it likely, do not you?"

Boru nodded to the soldiers and one took hold of Lauro while the other tied her hands behind her back.

She stood defiantly, her chin in the air. "So I am to be the sacrifice instead of her? A clever plan but I do not think it will save her. Borchard has a great alliance of houses planned. Do you think he will let you ruin that? For what? Your whore and the bastards she can give you to stand in his way? He has grown adamant over the years, oh yes, I have heard, adamant. I knew him before he grew brittle and cold, before Halduro and his poisoned words spread in him. Halduro steered him like a ship on a stormy sea to the safe haven of your mother's wealth and the harbor of her noble house. Oh yes, I knew them both, damn them. And if the general is dead...don't worry, there are other men just waiting who will gladly offer counsel. How long do you think she will remain alive? If she has a child they will see her and the babe killed to clear the field and 'protect' the legacy. I tell you, let Halduro lie in what ever shallow grave he has found...if that was his fate...and dig a grave for your heart as well. Return to your duties, Warrior, leave the girl alone and marry who ever you father orders you to."

"Take her out...make her ready to hang. Await my orders." Boru shouted and stormed out of the room.

"Warriors must fight...lambs must die, that is all they are good for..." she sang softly in a child-like voice as they dragged her out.

Brilla climbed the last steps to the veranda just as the soldiers pulled Lauro out into the sunshine. The wails of women and the pounding of their fists could be heard through the closed windows and doors. Brilla tried to free her from the soldiers but they pushed her roughly aside.

"Did you see Boru? What did he say? What did you tell him? E' cares noothin' for tha' devil, you know E' doon't. 'E was goin' ta call off the search. E' did'na care whether the bastard lived or died..." suddenly Brilla realized. "You hurt him didn't you! You shooed 'im away with yer high tone an' yer long nose! Ah know yer mind! Yah doon't care who yah hurt...if it's a man...How could you do to her what tha' bastard did to you?" Brilla shuffled along beside the soldiers as they moved to the edge of the balcony.

"What do you mean?" Lauro spoke through clenched teeth.

"Ya' tried ta' make 'im walk away from her...ah knew yah would! An' all tha' same thing happened ta you, or don't you remember?"

"He's The Guardian's son. He's a warrior."

"Yew an' yer fookin' warriors! That's all they are to you! Bloody black an' white brain of yours! But it don't work that way fer real people! It's her choice ta make...who she loves...not yours...not Jems's not even the captain's...hers!"

"How kind you are! How you defend her," Lauro leaned against the arms that held her, shouting at Brilla. "when you have no one...You little fool! They're all alike. He'll never marry her...she'll be killed! She'll suffer! She's a Giver! I tried to save her!"

"Aye...an' what about tha'?" Brilla whispered, coming in close. "Soomthin' else you left out of yer pretty speech to him, I'd bet my life on it!" Brilla spat on the ground. "She's havin' 'is babby an' you left tha' out, didn't you?"

"Let us say I told no lies. Why are you so determined to see them together in spite of what will happen to her? Oh, I see, I see." Lauro laughed sardonically. "You must want something...or someone...maybe the fisherman, you're just like me after all, aren't you, my pet? Hearts are fools, eh?"

"Ah'll never be like you!" Brilla screamed.

The guards wrenched Lauro away and pushed her up against the railing as Boru walked out upon the lawn near by. Brilla ran to him pointing at Lauro and the guards. One was fashioning a noose which he placed about Lauro's neck while the other tied the rope to one of the stone columns of the balustrade.

Brilla grabbed the lapels of Boru's jacket and begged him to listen to her while looking back and forth between him and the soldiers. He removed her hands and taking her

arm dragged her to a bench. Gradually he loosened his grip as she pleaded with him to listen. They sat for a long time while she spoke rapidly of Aolwynd and the child, of Lauro's troubled mind, of the matron's past love for his father and of Halduro's long history of treachery. When she had finished he held up his hand to the soldiers. She stood and beckoned him to the iron gate where they disappeared behind the cypress hedge.

The guards waited impatiently as Lauro leaned casually over the balustrade gazing at the sky, the sea and the beach below.

When Boru came out of the graveyard he bowed to Brilla and strode purposely toward the waiting guards. Suddenly he broke into a run as he heard women screaming and saw Lauro climbing up onto the stone railing by herself. The guards stood by as if all were going according to plan, watching her, one even offered his hand to help her up.

Brilla screamed, tripped as she ran and fell to the ground.

Lauro was staring back at them and smiling, her hair whipping about her head in the wind.

The sound of breaking glass made the guards turn as Cere, Lyla and the women patients came rushing out onto the veranda, but it was too late.

Boru motioned for the guards to hold the women back then ran to the balustrade and looked over the edge of the precipice. A crooked little figure lay at its base. The rope had snapped and it swung in the breeze against the side of the cliff, lifeless. On the beach below, the waves were lapping about Lauro's broken body, rocking it back and forth, playing against the shore.

22

With the Blade Uppermost

Mam was standing on the beach looking at a turbulent sea. The wind blew her skirts and ruffled the edges of her shawl as she hugged it closer about her. The clouds scudded across a darkening sky. "Storm's up." she muttered turning her bent back to the gusts and white caps that shoveled foam against the shore.

Coming along the beach was a horseman. Mam shaded her eyes. "E's either over-large or E's got two heads." she crowed as she scuttled up the bank and stood waiting in front of her cottage. The rider turned his horse toward the house. Mam squinted, waiting, as the first drops of rain began to fall.

"Mam!" Jem called grinning at her as he let the reins fall and jumped off the horse.

"Not another one? What av' you been up to?" she asked,

embracing her son.

"No time now, get 'er inside."

Aolwynd drooped over the horse's neck, wet and shivering.

"Poor lamb!" the old woman said taking hold of her as Jem pulled her down. "You're fair froze, lass."

"Mam...I'm so glad to see you..." Aolwynd's teeth chattered. A crack of thunder sent the women inside while Jem took the horse to the shed he'd built for Sprat, the pony.

The rain drummed against the cottage walls. Mam peeled the wet cloak off Aolwynd as she stood beside the hearth.

"Lawks! You've noothin' on but yer shift...no wonder yer froze. What's my son bin doin' to you?"

Jem spluttered his innocence and told his mother all that had happened through the bedroom door while Mam undressed her charge. When they came back out, Jem had built the fire to a roar and brought in more wood.

"There! Yah look a proper fisherman's wife now." Mam said proudly. Aolwynd teetered in the doorway, a timid smile on her face. She wore a short black wool skirt over a longer green underskirt topped by a white blouse and a black bodice cinched in tight a little above the waist.

Jem shook his head as if coming out of a dream and took his time admiring her. He lead her to a chair by the fire. Wrapping a blanket about her shoulders, he tucked it in beneath her legs so that he held her in his embrace, his face close to hers.

"You look good enoof ta' eat." he whispered.

"Jem..." she sighed.

"Doon't. Doon't say anythin'. It's alreet. I won't bother yah. Joost let me take care of yah. It's all I ask."

"I can't let you do that..."

"Yah must."

"Let 'er be Jem. Let 'er doze by the fire till supper. Yer both worn out...an' she's..." Mam said with a question on her lips. "Coom away. Get me some more wood."

Jem looked at the pile he'd already brought in but left the cottage obediently for more. "Don't argue with Mam..." he murmured.

"Tha's right..." Mam began. They stood outside in the wind with their heads together talking for a few moments. Aolwynd was too tired to care.

The wind began to howl. Waves that had merely slapped the shore an hour before were now curling, tall as a truculent child and throwing themselves against the seawalls of the other cottages. Black thunderclouds marched resolutely across the sky. Jem pulled his boat right up onto the sand and tipped it over, then ran down the beach to help others do the same.

The rain began to pelt his skin as he turned for home. It was then he noticed a horseman coming from the east with a woman riding pillion. The torrent and the darkness obscured his sight until they were nearly on top of him.

Boru reined in his mount. Brilla sat behind him. He jumped down and ran up to Jem slipping on the wet ground. "Where is she?"

Jem squinted at him through the rain and wiped his face. "I said, where is she?"

Jem looked up at Brilla then back at the captain. "She's no here." he said jutting out his jaw and crossing his arms over his chest.

Boru looked back at Brilla. She nodded her head slowly and looked toward the cottage.

"Jem...don't lie to me...don't stand in my way."

"Aye. I'm thinkin' I'll do just tha' from now on."

Boru sneered.

"I'm thinkin' I'll stand, an' I'll tell you somethin' fer

nothin'. Yer not good enoof fer her, nobleman! She's doon everythin' fer you, lost 'er Mam, lost 'er livelihood, near lost 'er life...what 'av you done fer her?"

"Get out of my way!" Boru shouted and made to push past him but Jem grabbed hold.

"No, you listen ta' me. Aye, you bedded 'er, that you did...but tha's all you did. I was there through it all, what she did fer your babby brother's sake. I killed tha' Banker bastard afore E' raped her. Did ye know tha' bit, nobleman? I got 'er out of the fire afore she burned ta' death like poor Gerda and we burned them ships together like she promised yew she would. If it weren't fer her an' me, yew'd still be starin' at that damned wall beggin' ta be let in!"

Boru winced at his words, then smiled grimly. "For the last time Jem...I don't want to hurt you...She's mine...and the child."

Jem's face took on a look of desperation, then a cruel smile flickered across his face. "What makes yew so sure that babby's yours?"

Boru's eyes widened for an instant and he looked as though he'd been slapped. Then as if a burden of obligation had been lifted from his shoulders that left him free to act, a simple solution came to him he knew all too well. He bore down on Jem in a fury and grabbed him about the neck.

Jem pushed him back and drew out his fisherman's knife. It was long and thin with a curved tip. Pointing the blade with his thumb on top he extended his arm and turned his body sideways so that the knife was closest to his enemy. Boru flashed his teeth and pulled out a dagger. He held up his hand for a moment, unclasped his heavy cloak of fur, now sodden with the rain, letting it drop to the ground.

Brilla gasped and digging her heels into the horse's flanks galloped off down the beach toward Mam's cottage.

Thunder roared around the sky and a bolt of lightning lit the two figures as they circled each other, watching for an awkward step or a lapse of attention, waiting for their chance to make the first cut.

They were equally matched in strength but Boru's technique showed years of training in close combat and the confidence that goes with it. He held his knife with his back hand and the blade uppermost, a more dangerous position but for a man of his ability ultimately giving him more power. He wheeled around and cut Jem lightly on the shoulder just to see what he was made of.

Jem only grimaced and set his jaw. He had no formal training outside of brawling at the local taverns, but all knife fights were deadly and he'd been in enough to know how to handle himself. Boru gained respect for him with the first cut. Jem fought with passion and a recklessness of purpose that belied his quiet demeanor.

The captain stepped back out of range to wipe his eyes. The rain was coming down in sheets now. He tripped on a rock only just managing to stay out of the way of Jem's blade. Grabbing his shoulder and closed his eyes for a split second. The wounds from his last battle had re-opened but he clambered to his feet. Consumed by fury he felt no pain. Jem stood waiting for him to get up, gasping for air and blinking away the rain.

Lightning flashed somewhere down the strand, this time illuminating three women running toward the fight.

The men circled again, blades gleaming in the lightning strike as they moved back and forth, slashing and jabbing at each other. Boru sliced again, cutting Jem across the chest. The wet linen of the fisherman's shirt turned pink, then red from blood as it fanned out across the fabric, clinging to his

skin.

Aolwynd stumbled up to them, crying and with a frantic look at Brilla threw herself between them.

"Get back luv..." Jem shouted turning toward her, exposing his back.

Boru's dagger slid easily across Jem's ribs leaving a long gash, but the warrior held his blade steady not letting it travel further into the flesh. It was enough. Aolwynd grabbed Jem about the waist and pulled him aside as he began to fall onto the sand.

At that moment two arrows flew past them and one found its home in Aolwynd's back. She fell forward onto the ground covering Jem with her body.

The women screamed.

Boru cried out in anguish but swung around instinctively, passing his dagger to his other hand and drawing his sword, ready in an instant to fight this new assailant, who ever it might be.

Coming up the beach was a troop of soldiers and archers with the standard of The Supreme Guardian flying above them. Borchard was at the head of the column and an archer rode by his side, bow in hand.

Ten soldiers jumped from their saddles and with swords drawn they surrounded Jem and Aolwynd.

Boru stood gulping for air, his sword arm hanging loose at his side, a dark stain seeping below the skirt of his leather jacket onto his breeches.

Brilla swore an oath and tried to push her way through the guards, pounding on their backs. "Let me through! By the Gods! I'm from the House of Good Women!"

Borchard gestured his assent, riding his horse up to them and the soldiers parted to let her inside.

Mam stumbled about outside the circle of men peering over shoulder after shoulder, weeping.

The Guardian dismounted and walked up to his son, threw his arms about him and breathed into his ear, "Enough." He held out his hand for Boru's sword and took it away, guiding his son's faltering steps toward a horse. "Enough, my warrior."

Boru cradled his arm against his chest, gasping with pain at every breath and rested his forehead against the neck of the animal.

"What do you wish us to do with these, my lord? Is this the woman?" asked a soldier. Borchard looked at his son for guidance but could see only despair and exhaustion in his eyes.

After a moment Boru held up his head. "She is already dead, the woman you're after. Let these others go. There is no one here we want." he whispered. Borchard gave the order.

The guards sheathed their swords as one man, turned and removed themselves from around the huddled figures. Re-mounting their horses, they rode about the group on the beach in a tight circle as if to flaunt their martial authority and rejoined the column ready to leave.

Borchard made a stirrup of his own hands and helped his son into the saddle. It was then he noticed the jacket now soaked with blood. The stitching Lauro had so carefully sewn into Boru's flesh had re-opened and pulled apart during the fight. Boru seemed in a daze and quietly obeyed his father's tender instructions. Boru fell forward against the horse's neck and held the pommel for support.

Borchard rode close beside his son, holding the reins and guiding the horse slowly away from the beach. Looking back, the Guardian's face was stoney as he gestured to his men. The troop moved away, scattering sand and water in their wake. The rain had stopped and a sick yellow light was breaking through below the clouds but the sea was still violent.

Brilla helped Jem to his feet and stripped the torn and bloody shirt from his back. The cuts were long, yet clean and not too deep, grazing his ribs but miraculously, passing over the spine. He would heal well. Boru had not wanted to kill him, and surely could have, she thought.

Aolwynd lay unconscious on the sand, her knees curled up to her stomach, drenched through and blue from the rain and the cold.

"Help me get her up." Brilla said but before she could stop him, Jem had picked up his love and was carrying her down the beach. He walked with the wind to his back trying to spare the treasure in his arms. Blood trickled from his open wound and Brilla noticed the sand crusted there. She was already making plans to wash it away and thinking about the arrow in Aolwynd's back and what she must do next.

The wind was powerful and the women's skirts clung to their legs propelling them like sails as they struggled down the strand to the cottage.

23

By a Loop of Ribbon Bound

Mam loped along with long strides, arriving first and flinging the cottage door open, got her medicine chest. She dragged out a mattress and laid it down by the fire.

Jem laid Aolwynd down on her stomach and Brilla set about cutting away the bodice, belt and blouse.

"She's with us still, but it's just as well she's out, this is going to hurt." Brilla said. She braced her hand flat against Aolwynd's bare back with the arrow between her thumb and forefinger. With all the delicacy she could muster she grasped the shaft, wriggling it ever so slightly to see if it had lodged in bone and having made sure this was not the case she said,

"Let's hope it hasna' pierced the lung." She gave a mighty growl of exertion and pulled it straight up through the flesh. Aolwynd made a noise like a child. Brilla handed the arrow to Mam.

"I'll burn tha' evil thing." she said.

"No, keep it." Jem whispered.

Mam handed Brilla a cloth, for as soon as the arrow was free the puncture bled profusely.

"We'll soon know how deep. Hold this down till it stops bleeding while I see to Jem." Brilla said.

He was sitting astride a chair with his arms resting on the back, his head down and his legs spread out before him. Brilla took a cloth, soaked it and carefully trickled water over the wound to dislodge the sand. When it was clean she wrapped him tightly in yard after yard of bandage that Mam had cut from a sheet. She tried not to touch him even as she saw to his wound for even now, even seeing how much he loved Aolwynd, Brilla was saddened and ached for a love of her own. It was not jealousy she told herself, nor lust. Her fate, like Lauro's, sealed by their oath to the goddess, alone and married to her vocation, seemed assured now, no hope. She gulped back bitter emotions, pushing the hair out of her eyes as she worked.

Wrapping clean moss in a bandage she went back to the fire and placed the pad on Aolwynd's back. Jem held her upright as Brilla wrapped her chest in bandages as well. Then they laid her down and pulled off the sodden skirts. She looked like a toddler curled up with her slightly swollen belly. They covered her with blankets but her lips were still blue. Jem climbed in next to her, holding her close. He could not be persuaded to move. He waved the fussing women away and laid his strong arm over Aolwynd, closing his eyes.

"Oh, let the man be." Mam said finally, taking a bottle of brandy out of a cupboard and placing two cups made of shell on the table. Brilla held out her cup and downed the first drink like an old soldier. She sat looking at the pair on the floor without saying a word, only holding out her cup to Mam when it was empty. The two women sat across from each other the rest of the night drinking until they fell asleep. Brilla did not have to speak, Mam knew all her secrets by the look of her.

In the morning they found Jem sitting up and holding his love in his arms rocking her back and forth while murmuring something into her ear. There was a smile on her face, her eyes were sleepy and for the first time her cheeks had color in them. Aolwynd reached out her hand when Brilla raised her head from the table. "Thank you, my love, for so many things."

Brilla held her forehead, groaned and coughed. "E's like a big bloody sheepdog, init? You can't get loose of 'im."

"Nothing to be done..."

"Best keep 'im then, I guess." Brilla said going to the window and brushing aside the curtain to hide her feelings. "Gods! It's bright. Storm's over." she muttered.

"You'll be alreet now, yer makin' jokes." Jem said.

Aolwynd reached up to stroke his cheek and tears flooded her eyes. It was all she could manage before she fell back against him, exhausted.

Mam kept the cottage dark and warm and shooed away the neighbors from her door. Many of the fisherfolk had seen the troops and the fight and wanted to know what had happened. She dragged them away and proudly told the whole tale as best she could.

Brilla tended them both until one morning Jem sat Aolwynd up in a chair and dragged the mattress back into the bedroom. He handed his mother her few possessions and helped her set up a bed in the kitchen. Then he moved Aolwynd, tucked her in to bed and put his shoes beneath it.

Brilla raised her eyebrows and looked at Mam. Mam

only smiled and said "As it should be."

Jem thanked Brilla. "Take the horse, go home." he whispered gently.

Brilla huffed and puffed something about pregnant women needing their own kind and the comforts of the hospice but finally she kissed them all goodbye and went back to the city.

When he wasn't fishing, Jem was loath to let even his Mam tend to Aolwynd. He brought her meals, washed her, changed her bandages and helped her sit on the pot to relieve herself.

As the days went by Aolwynd surrendered and came to hunger for Jem's voice, for his touch and could not sleep unless his arms were around her at night. She worried until he was safe from the sea and out of his boat. When she gave birth his hands were waiting to catch the child and welcome him into the world. Her smile mirrored his and she gained back her strength feeding on his love.

As they lay together one night after the birth of the child she whispered to him, "Take me home."

Jem hitched a cart to the pony the very next morning and put the mattress in the back. He and Mam helped her in, laid the baby next to her and rode away from the sea.

Aolwynd watched the clouds above her as she had done in the Good Women's cart after the battle for the garrison. It seemed long ages ago. As they climbed the cliff road and drew close to the inn, Jem shouted back to her, "Look there! Yer father's waiting at the gate!"

Aolwynd started to cry. They pulled into the courtyard and Jem picked her up and walked forward but before depositing her in her father's arms he whispered in her ear, "Ah'm not leavin' you, not ever, so you'd best marry me an' teach me 'ow ta run this here inn. I'll never make a soldier,

258

nor a 'Good Woman' neither. Ahm not leavin' you nor the babby even if I 'av ta play that wicked old man's game every night fer the rest of me life."

She closed her eyes, nodded and reached out for her father.

As the years went by, many changes took place. The city of Saels built watch towers along the coast. The Guardian promised more frequent patrols and increased his communication with his far flung provinces.

Brilla went back to the House of Good Women and finding Lauro's notes, studied the healing arts as best she could, becoming head of the order in time. She lavished attention on the men's ward until they were no longer treated only to be patched up and sent off but cared for as tenderly as the women patients were.

Mam moved into the inn and took over Gerda's kitchen when it re-opened as if she had always been there. She added seafood to most of Gerda's recipes and her chowder became famous throughout the region.

The inn prospered and Jorus re-carved the sign out front adding the likeness of an arrow beneath the swan.

Aolwynd's father lived to teach Jem a good game of Kings Men and to see his other two grandchildren born, although his health took a turn at first when he learned of Gerda's death. He was never as strong as before his spirit was the same.

Jem and Aolwynd were married in a great local celebration. Folpas, Mam, Jorus and the household stood behind the couple on the steps of the inn as Jem tied a ribbon of red leather about Aolwynd's wrist. Mam said a prayer before the crowd of neighbors and it was done. Tables were set in the courtyard and the city folk, fisherfolk and their families all came for the feast. There were heaps of clams and mussels in a black sauce made from the ink of squids and crabs steaming in a cauldron over an open fire pit. Flagons of mead and ale were hoisted into the air and the children had cider and pastries filled with roasted apples dipped in honey.

There were many songs and poems sung late into the night, and some new ones about pirates, the burning of the ships and the gallant Guardian's son who had saved them all. The bride grew quiet while listening to this ballad of many stanzas. Jem took her hand and begged them to change the tune, whispering in her ear, "In this world yah either dance or cry, dance or cry."

Jorus took up his lute and strummed apace until the musicians quickened their instruments and the dancing began. The couple danced first and last beneath the white blossoms of the pear tree till dawn came.

Aolwynd and Jem had three children. Their first born, Boru, had light brown hair that hung to his shoulders and piercing blue eyes. He was brusque and reckless, with a smile that could "melt the mountaintops of snow" Jem said. He was constantly in trouble but his mother called him her "Little Eagle" and never scolded him but only held him close.

Their second son Jors, named after their beloved gardener, had black curly hair and dark eyes exactly like Jem's. His demeanor was quiet and thoughtful. He loved the sea and spent hours picking up treasures along the shore or fishing for urchins among the rocks while his older brother played at sword fighting with sticks and raced along the strand yelling and slicing the air.

Their third child was a girl, Brilliana. Her hair was also dark and she wore it in a long plait down her back that swung when she walked. Her brothers liked to tease her, especially Boru, who was her favorite, for he longed for far off places as did she. They were always roaming about the hillsides together watching the clouds and daydreaming. Boru often carried her on his back to the cliffs and pointed out the ships as they passed telling her they would sail away together one day on a great adventure.

24

"Would You Follow Me...?"

One day young Boru and Brillie were standing in the middle of the road on the hillside above the inn looking west toward the city. A troop of soldiers came up behind them riding fast. Boru grabbed his little sister's hand and dashed out of their way.

A captain dressed in green with a labyrinth emblazoned on his tunic rode up alongside his column and stopping, inquired of the children if there was "...an inn in these parts?" His face was weary from long travel, yet he seemed pleased and surprised to see the children.

Young Boru looked up into the man's face and smiled broadly. "The Swan and Arrow is my father's house and the best inn for miles around. You would be made most welcome there." He pointed to the villa at the bottom of the

hill. The guardian grinned and mirrored his smile so
exactly, jutting his chin out in the same way as the boy that
Boru became uneasy. He had seen that same face staring
back at him countless times from pools and streams. Brillie
grew shy and confused looking up at the handsome stranger
and then at her brother. 'Surely this is family.' she thought
with her quick child's mind.

"And is this the Swan of that name?" The soldier asked
the little girl, turning his brilliant blue eyes on her and
covering his heart with his hand.

"Nay...tha's m' little sister Brilliana." Boru mumbled
losing interest.

"Ah...it's been a long time..." the man said. Suddenly
standing up in his stirrups, his hand shading his gaze, he
searched the inn and its courtyard. "and how far is it to the
city?" he asked distractedly. The man seemed suddenly
nervous, excited.

"Aboot anoother few mile." Boru was getting bored
with the stranger's questions and looking with lust in his
heart at the armor, the banner and the man's sword. "Can I
see yer sword? I want to be a soldier like you when I'm
grown...!" he dismissed with a shrug the laughter he heard
coming from the other soldiers.

"Do you?" Their leader studied his face carefully, then
looked again at the inn.

A woman had come out of the house and stood in the
courtyard. She held a basket of laundry on one hip and was
shading her eyes with the other hand, looking up toward the
hill.

"What's yer horses' name?" Boru asked.

"Pirate." The man said softly. He was clearly only half-
listening to what the boy was asking. His gaze was riveted
on the woman standing there.

"Take me with you!" Brillie suddenly blurted out with

passion, catching hold of the man's stirrup. She clung to it with both her little hands, jerking it and slapping his foot against his horse's flank. She looked up at him with beady eyes, demanding his attention.

He turned to her. She gasped and hiccuped. There was something terribly hurt in his expression like a dog told to go away. Those eyes she knew so well had looked back at her over the dinner table every night begging for her last bite of cake. Her brother's eyes. She sucked in her breath.

The man sat back in the saddle for a few moments and sighed. Searching her face he leaned down and took her chin gently in his hand. She could not catch his gaze, for he was looking past her at the inn and he whispered, not quite in her ear but almost beseems to someone else, "Would you follow me, then? Little fool."

Brillie jumped back at the gentle tickle of his breath and let go of the stirrup. "Who are you?" she exclaimed. "Are you my uncle? How do you know tha' joke of Dah's? 'E teases 'er with it all the time." Then as explanation she added, "Me moother says tha' when she stands on this hill, right here, where we're standin', fer years an' years she's said it, lookin' yer way, back where you came from. What do it mean? Do you know?"

Straightening up suddenly the guardian sat back in his saddle and gripped the reins tightly in his hand. She saw his knuckles turn white as he did so. It was as if he'd woken up from a dream.

"We'd better push on." he called to the men behind him. With his eyes still searching the now empty courtyard he signaled the column to ride forward, then turned his gaze toward the city.

The children jumped as the horses galloped past them.

Brillie ran after them until she faltered and stopped. She stood on the crest and cried as they disappeared from sight.

End of Volume One,
The Tales of Earden,
The Swan and Arrow

The story continues in
The Fledgling
Volume Two

About the Author

J. Carter Merwin was born to a pair of avid readers. She grew up on Dickens, Dumas, Scott, Shakespeare, Alcott, Austen...all the classics. Amongst all these 'good works' were the modern adventure novels of Thomas B. Costain (her father's favorite) and Daphne Du Maurier, (her mother's). She has illustrated and published her own works and those of others through her publishing company MacGregor House.

She lives in a relatively quiet college town (at least during the school breaks) in Central Vermont and runs a small gallery there featuring the oil paintings of her artist husband, Tom, her own pen and ink work and the video artistry of her son. McGregor House Publishing, her indie imprint is housed there also.

In addition, she worked for many years at the Rutland County Humane Society of Vermont and during that time proudly and lovingly cared for over 12.000 animals. A portion of the profits of these books go to that organization. She has one dog and four cats.

www.ingramcontent.com/pod-product-compliance
Lightning Source LLC
Chambersburg PA
CBHW032024240626
47154CB00003B/772